Frenchie's Best Friend

Follow the Blog

by Mary L. Laudien

TWOCANDO BOOKS
WEST VANCOUVER, BRITISH COLUMBIA
CANADA

ISBN-10: 145643358X
ISBN-13: 9781456433581
LCCN: 2010918414

Library and Archives Canada Cataloguing in Publication

Laudien, Mary, 1954-
Frenchie's best friend : follow the blog / Mary Laudien.

I. Title.

PS8623.A8175F74 2011   jC813'.6   C2011-900127-6

Library of Congress Cataloguing-in-Publication Data

TwoCanDo Books
West Vancouver, British Columbia
Canada
Printed in the USA

This story was inspired by my sons and their partners (Étienne and Kelsey, Adrien and Kasia) because of the passion they demonstrate for my French Bulldog "grand dogs" - Bert and Cecile.

Table of Contents

1

Welcome to Ethan's World

I'm what you might call "dog crazy." I daydream about French Bulldogs, I read about them, I seek them out on the sea wall, I cruise the Internet advertising homes for them, I even dream about them at night. Maybe I could be called obsessed—I know that's what my mom believes! So why, you ask, do I not have a Frenchie of my own? The answer, my friends, is pure and simple—I'm not allowed. That's right. I'm in eighth grade and my mother still will not let me have a dog. She comes up with every excuse imaginable.

It is really all about her these days. She calls herself a "single mom" now that my dad has moved on (meaning he decided to "take a break" from the routine of family life after about twenty years and moved away to Vancouver Island to *find* himself). Apparently he's still looking because he didn't come back (to our family, that is), but he has started a new career and lives permanently over there. That's okay, because, as a child of divorced parents, I get to visit him in Victoria and spend time with his dogs. He and "his new partner in life" have a couple of Westies.

Anyways, like I was saying, now that my mom is a "single parent," she believes she has to have strict control over everything that involves me. Her strongest argument is that she works long hours at school and it would be unkind to leave a dog home alone for an endless day. What she doesn't get is that Grandpa Bob, who lives on the next block would gladly squeeze a pee break in for his "grand dog" between his golf games and bridge. I know he would. And on the odd day that he couldn't, I would jog home for lunch and let him out. I could easily make it in the forty-five minutes we have for lunch break.

Mom always says that if I love dogs so much, then I should just spend more time caring for Grandma Sis' and Grandpa Bob's puppy, Cher. She's a Bichon Frisé, and Grandma Sis believes she's a glamorous dog because of her fluffy puffy coat. Grandma chose the name Cher as she (not so secretly) believes that she, herself, resembles the old movie star and singer, Cher. I've looked really closely at pictures of Cher and I have to be honest, if there is a similarity, it has to be that they are both really tall…. Anyways, it's not that I don't like their dog Cher, I do, but she isn't exactly a guy's kind of dog; I mean really, what guy is going to want to be seen with a fussy little white "foo foo" dog?! When I think of a French Bulldog, I picture a heavyset, sturdy "little man" with whom to wrestle and walk around town, not some little "fluff ball!" A Frenchie is an affectionate breed, and they're hilarious because of being so front heavy and lacking balance. Never throw a Frenchie off a boat into the ocean—for sure he would sink! Their personalities are adorable, they're such a comical breed. Nothing is funnier than to watch them lay down with their back legs stretched out behind them— they look so incredibly cute!

Mom always says I have enough responsibility around home with keeping my room tidy, unloading the dishwasher, mowing the lawn, and keeping up with my homework; without adding a dog into the mix. She can't understand how I have time after school (before she gets home) to get all my homework done. Little does she realize (until she gets my report card) that in actuality, I'm not really doing much homework. The TV and computer seem to be a deterrent to my intellectual development. She doesn't know this, as she is so immersed in school, she just thinks everyone else "lives and breathes" education. It's going to be a rude awakening when first term reports come out! I think it's safe to say that I'm somewhat of a disappointment to my mom in this matter already. She just can't accept the fact that her Grade Eight son is just not that academically inclined. She believes everyone has "smarts," but I think she's still trying to pinpoint what exactly mine are! Getting good marks at school are really not a big motivator for me. I seem to get by through making conscious choices. That's right, I'm good at reading people and making sure I'm in the right classes where the teachers are more open-minded about their practices. This means they prefer to teach kids through inquiry and let us research during class with laptops, as well as work in collaboration with a team. I know how to pick my friends for these opportunities. I always finesse it so that I'm with one or two of those kids who have the language "smarts." That means they're great writers and communicators. It seems to be helping me glide through without any major stress. Maybe I'm not the next Einstein, but I'm doing okay. So, Mom's argument about me not having time for any more responsibility, like taking care of a dog, really doesn't cut it. Now I just have to convince her!

My dad always sticks up for me when it comes to having my own pet. He reminds my mom about how I must feel coming home to an empty house every day (just a little guilt trip to make her feel bad for being such a workaholic) and how a dog would be a comfort to me. As far as being an advocate, Dad is pretty persuasive (he should be—that's his business to promote stocks that no one really wants to buy), but unfortunately where my dad is concerned, my mom can become obstinate. She would never want anyone to think that she agreed with anything he suggested. Now, if he had played it the other way and refused to even discuss the idea of a pet for me—I might have had a fighting chance.

Another big obstacle in my mother's mind is the cost of buying a purebred dog and its vet bills. She says it's fine for my dad to have a zoo at his house (three cats and two dogs), but on a teacher's salary, there's no way we could swing the financial burden of the upkeep for a dog. She always comes back to the horror stories she hears from her colleagues and families about how they are spending more on their dog's vet bills than on their mortgage payments some months. She believes, in her conservative way, that one does not burden one's family financially for any reason—and especially for a dog that we don't have time to look after, anyways. It's really hard to dissuade her when she's off on this kind of a tangent. She always seems to win that argument. What do people always say—it always comes down to *MONEY*! Well, I'm going to figure out how to get enough of it, so she isn't going to be able to use that argument against me any longer.

And that's where Grandma Sis comes in. She's probably the most interesting grandma that any kid could have. First of all, as Mom puts it, she "marches to her own drum." That's an old fashioned way to say she is true to herself.

Like I said before, she believes she looks like that old star Cher, and so, to add to her appearance, Grandma Sis wears shorts over her pantyhose every day of the year with high heels. She says it shows off her long legs. I personally have trouble explaining to my friends why she's wearing shorts in the middle of winter, to say nothing about the pantyhose with which she is trying to disguise her varicose veins. It kind of "creeps us guys out" to see an old lady dressed like that. My mom says to just get over it; that's part of what makes her unique. Whatever!

Now you have to know my grandma and grandpa are in their mid seventies, and neither one has a gray hair on their heads. Grandma was a hair stylist, and she believes it is sinful to have gray hair. Every Sunday afternoon, she and Grandpa give each other a dye job. It's hilarious to see the reddish brown dye sitting on Grandpa's thinning scalp, but they think they look great for their age, and Mom says that's all that matters.

Grandma is not your typical "let me make you cookies" kind of grandma. (Are you getting the picture?) In my younger years, when my babysitter had to have an emergency operation, Grandma was enlisted to let me spend my after-school hours with her, until my mom could make it home from work. Let me tell you, it was always an adventure! Either I would walk in on a coffee party with "her ladies" (whose hair she still styles the same way, frozen in time, in her basement mini-salon) and they would be gossiping about the latest issues on *Oprah*, sex scandals of the stars on *Entertainment Tonight* and all those other forbidden shows.... Or she would have her favorite soap story going and invite me to watch it with her. *The Young and the Restless* is one she never misses. There's a TV in every room in her house—I kid you not! When I came home and told my mom that Victor got another woman pregnant, my mom didn't think this was exactly the most appropriate environment for a six year old. Grandma was never asked to babysit me again!

What I like about Grandma Sis is that she's kind of devious in a cool sort of way. She always thinks that everyone believes everything she says, but when you know her like we do, you realize she tells a lot of little white lies. Mom says it's probably because she grew up in such a big family, and when you have so many other siblings to compete with, you might sometimes do some dishonest things to set yourself apart and get what you want and need. It's not like she is a bad person, but she will lie if she thinks she can provoke you (meaning, "get you going") or she thinks it will have the effect of making you feel better and not hurt your feelings. She doesn't exactly tell you the straight goods on most things, if you know what I mean. It's just kind of a habitual personality flaw that she has. Mom gets super annoyed when she pulls this on her, because she sees it as manipulation. She knows that whatever we tell Grandma Sis about personal things, she will pass directly onto her son (my dad) and that just makes it hard for Mom to trust her. Mom doesn't really want Dad involved in our day-to-day decisions, as she feels he lost that privilege when he "moved on." I get that and try not to upset her, but the dog may have to be an exception, as I think I'll need Grandma's "gifts" to help me get my dog.

All I can say is that one has to admire Grandma Sis' spirit, her sense of fun, and her ability to make money. She has a business head, and I would like to think that maybe just a little of that has rubbed off on me. She loves to make some fast cash and is always scheming about ways to augment her old-age pension (that's how she puts it). For example, one summer, she made Grandpa Bob so upset because she bought up all of these used fridges and stored them in his garage. He couldn't get his car or his lawn mower in or out of it, it was so jammed. Then she put an ad in the paper to sell them to people for their cottages at the lake. He wasn't quite so upset when she booked their trip to Maui with the profits from her quick-cash scheme. This is just one of many of her successful moneymaking plans. In fact, Grandpa Bob never knows who is going to be sitting at the breakfast table. She gets wind of special events happening in town, and the next thing he knows, she has a house full of paying guests rotating through their extra bedrooms. She loves the company (although she isn't a registered "bed and breakfast"), and she has all that extra, non-taxable cash coming in. I like her entrepreneurial spirit and I hope to emulate her skills one day.

So, what you know about me thus far is that I'm totally "gaga" over French Bulldogs and I like to think I have a little business sense (from Grandma Sis). Although I may not be the successful academic student my mom would prefer I was, I think I have other "smarts," which you will eventually pick up on as I uncover the rest of my story. Now, you may be wondering, where is this leading? Well, hold on, dear readers, because I have quite a tale for you that may just inspire you to follow your very own passion, as well (*or not*)!

An "A-HA" Moment

Dad was in town on business that week and we hooked up at Grandma Sis' to have dinner together. I always feel a little weird about telling my mom that we're having dinner together—it's like she's being left out or something. I guess it will always be this way, even though she says she isn't mad at Dad, it's clear that she is hurt by his actions (in her words). I think that when he got remarried, that really "shut the door for her." She pretty much wanted to describe Dad's "moving on" up to that point as just an immature phase he was going through, but I think Grandma Sis and Grandpa Bob knew it was the real thing, and he wasn't ever going to come back to live with us. So life moved ahead and my mom became more buried than ever in her work as an educator, and I have these occasional "somewhat-guilty visits" with my dad. My mom doesn't try to make me feel like I'm disappointing her by being with my dad; in fact, she always justifies it with, "Oh great, Ethan, that means I can stay later at school and catch up on some of my work."

I just wish she would take the opportunity to go out and do something fun with her girlfriends, instead. Dad says it's just a transition and she's still getting used to being single again, and it could take awhile before she "gets her wings." Grandma Sis thinks she is way too serious and needs to get on with dating. "The world is her oyster and there are lots of pots out there that are looking for lids." Really, really corny stuff like that, but as Mom says, Grandma Sis is a flirt, and she doesn't realize that there are piles of toads out there before you can meet a prince. Honestly, I'm just as glad that my mom isn't particularly looking at the opposite sex—I think it would gross me out somehow to think my mom was seeking a boyfriend. I mean, can you imagine if your mother was setting up dates on one of those Internet sites? No, I'll just stay content with the status quo for the time being. When would she have time to fit a man into her life anyways? She has me and her work and, as she puts it, "It's full on!"

So I went to dinner with Dad at Grandma Sis'. Did I mention that she is an incredible cook, as well as a great business head? She made Dad's favorites—roast chicken and apple pie for dessert. As we were making our way through dessert, the subject of "French Bulldogs" came up, don't ask *me* how! Anyways, I started in, once again, about all the reasons why ownership of one would be the ultimate and how ready I was to take on the responsibility. My dad wanted to jump right in and solve the issue by buying a Frenchie for me and weathering the storm with my mom from his safe haven on the Island. I explained that, as much as I appreciated the offer, it wouldn't be worth the insanity that I would endure when Mom "hit the roof" over his involvement. He backed down quite quickly, acknowledging that he wasn't in the best of positions to cross my mother on her decisions. We all heartily agreed that he needed to stay far away from any controversy that would bring out my mother's wrath.

The conversation took a turn and we started to discuss how the pet industry had really taken off in the last couple of years. You can't go anywhere these days that there aren't Big Box Pet Stores or Doggy Boutiques. On the news the other night, they showed a clip of a Doggie Hotel where the downtown yuppies drop off their dogs when they go on vacation. The dogs get spa treatments during their stay, flat screen TVs in their rooms, and Skype sessions in the evenings so that their owners (parents?) can say goodnight to them. There was also mention of the doggie restaurant that opened up in downtown Vancouver. The dogs sit at tables and they have organic meals to choose from. My mom gets upset when I tell her about all of this, as she has some kids at her school who don't even arrive in the morning with breakfast. It frustrates her to think that dogs get this kind of pampering when little children are neglected and hungry. She is right, of course, but what are we supposed to do about it? I agree that it might be just a little over the top, but being as dog crazy as I am, I can understand why people get a little "nutso" over their pets. I would want to spoil my dog, too.

Dad mentioned that he takes his Westies to a Dog Spa. They receive specialized treatments for their coats and get pedicures and a blow dry. He admitted it is a little costly, but everyone raves about this particular Doggie Salon on the Island, and it is worth every cent to have the dogs feeling gorgeous and pampered. I looked over at Grandma Sis, and I could see that certain sparkle in her eye that I knew meant she was scheming. She started asking questions like what kind of qualifications did these groomers have? What kind of facility was the shop housed in? What services did they provide and how much did each service cost the dog owner? I could see her business mind just getting ramped up, and I was starting to follow where she was going with this. Dad also mentioned that the salon sold various products (not foods), but clothing items (like hoodies, plaid raincoats, etc.) and some doggie jewelry. This piqued our interest, and he explained that all dogs wear collars, but now these collars are becoming necklaces made out of special metals or beads. By this time, both Grandma and I were visualizing the gold mine of opportunities out there, just waiting for us!

And thus, this became the night that my plan began to take shape. Of course, Dad and Grandpa Bob were completely clueless that Grandma Sis and I were already projecting cash coming our way. I knew from that night on that I was going to realize my dream and my Frenchie was only a few business months away.

3

A Plan is Hatched

When I got home that night, my mind was racing. Did I have the nerve to make a business happen without confiding in my mom? I just knew that if I asked her about it, she would come up with a zillion reasons why I was too young to do this. She wouldn't understand that I couldn't live any longer without having my own French Bulldog and that I was willing to work for it. I would not be denied! She would argue that it would take away from my studies—little did she realize that I wasn't actually spending much out of school time on schoolwork. My mom functions pretty much in the world of academia, and I knew that if I planned this properly, she wouldn't really clue in to what I was doing with my time between three-thirty and six o'clock each day. She rarely got home before six-thirty every night, and when she did get home, she always had that dazed, overwhelmed look on her face that said she was still bringing "it" home with her and struggling over her next steps to help little Eddie learn to read or how to deal with irate Suzie's father who thinks she's being bullied by the popular girls in her class, and the list goes on.... Quite honestly, my mom loves me and all, but even though she's dedicating her life to me, she really gives her all during the day at school and doesn't have that much more left by the time she makes her way home. This was going to work in my favor, as I was pretty sure that she was going to be oblivious to my new extracurricular activities.

My mom isn't really keen about the social networking aspects of technology—meaning she has a lot of hassles with kids misusing Facebook and email. Cyber bullying is a topic that she is constantly struggling with at school. She is adamant about knowing what I am using the computer for, and there are strict rules about its usage. The problem is, that for all she knows about the dangers, she really doesn't get it as a tool that every living human being in the world is now investing a majority of time in. At high school, we're being encouraged to use digital literacy through Twitter, blogs, Wikis, Texting, and Instant Messaging. I just seemed to pick it up by osmosis, and blogging was becoming my new pastime (mostly when Mom was at work). Up until now, all I had to blog about was French Bulldogs and share any stories I had about them from my research of the breed. I suddenly had a new purpose—I already knew I was going to blog my way through the entire process of acquiring my own Frenchie. This adventure was going to be shared with the world, and who knew, maybe someone would want to pick up my journey's story for a movie or a book—stranger things have happened (remember the movie about Julia Child, *Julie and Julia*?). That very night I started my blog—*"Frenchie's Best Friend."*

BLOG of Day 1

Hello all of you French Bulldog lovers out there in cyberland. Tonight is
the beginning of a journey that I can't
imagine any other Grade Eight student
has ever embarked upon. That's right,
an idea was hatched tonight for how I
would get around my mother's objections
about having my own French Bulldog and,
in the process, develop my own business. Yep, I am determined to under-
mine my mom's "barriers of entry" into
the world of dog ownership. She won't
know about the business until it's too
late and I have earned enough money to
buy my own dog and sustain the expenses that dog ownership incurs. By the
time this happens, I will have proven
to her that I am responsible and more
than mature enough to manage dog ownership. She won't have a "leg to stand
on" when it comes to objecting to the
idea—it will be a done deal. Well, dear
readers, more about this in the days to
come. Stay tuned.

Determined and Entrepreneurial,
Frenchie's Best Friend

I went to bed that night knowing that I needed to get
over to Grandma Sis' place right away after school to start
putting our plan in motion. It felt exhilarating to know that

I was getting started, and nothing was going to stop me now—I knew what had to be done. And having a co-conspirator was going to be a big plus when it came to making it all happen. How lucky a guy was I to have such a conniving grandma as my "partner in crime?"

Partners in Crime

Over breakfast the next morning, I couldn't help but broach the subject of dog ownership with my mom. It was all I could think about, and I really felt she should get one more final chance to come through on this and make me a dog owner. You can't fault me for trying.

"Hey, Mom, guess what kind of puppy Mike's family is going to buy this weekend?"

"Ethan, I have no idea; I know they already have a Golden Retriever, why in the world would they be buying another dog?" she asked.

"You just don't get it, Mom, do you? Do you realize that almost every one of my friends has at least one pet? Mike's mom is going back to work part-time, and she doesn't want their dog to be lonely, so they're getting a new puppy to be a playmate for Goldie. Saturday, they drive out to their dog breeders to pick out their new retriever. I think it's an awesome idea!" I informed her.

"Yes of course you do, Ethan, and if I had the luxury of just working a few hours each week, maybe I might even consider getting you a dog, but unless I win the Lottery—that isn't going to happen anytime soon," she retorted.

"You know, Mom, I really think you should reconsider me having a Frenchie. They are such good company, and you would know that I wasn't home alone after school, so you wouldn't have to feel so bad about being away such long hours at work and having me grow up as a latch-key kid," I begged.

"Nice try, Ethan. I'm not about to be *guilted* into letting you have a dog. You forget that I'm just trying to give us a life and save up enough for you to go to university. There's no way I can contend with the added burden of caring for a dog. So be fair about this and quit hounding me!" she pleaded.

"You know I would take care of the dog and you wouldn't have to lift a finger. And give me a break, Mom, I haven't ever told you that I'm prepared to become a university graduate. I know school is your life, but it doesn't necessarily mean that it's going to be mine."

"I don't understand how two university graduates could have raised a son with so little educational motivation. I knew from first grade that I was going to be an educator—it was in my blood. What in the world is going to get you moving, Ethan?" she asked.

"Mom, you might be surprised to find out what motivates me. I'd have to say money works for me. I can have freedom to do what I want to do, if I have enough cash," I answered.

"Well, Ethan, you may have a rude awakening one of these days when you realize that money doesn't come without a lot of effort and hard work. I think life lessons may be heading your way. Now finish your cereal and let's get moving, we both have a full day ahead of us."

I knew this conversation would have little effect, but I had to give her one more chance before I set my plan in motion, now, didn't I? I felt totally "buzzed" about getting things moving; it was going to be a GREAT day! She couldn't believe how I bounced out the door to get into the car for school! This was a totally rare occurrence, as you can imagine.

Arriving early to school gives me some time to "hang" with my friends before classes begin. Everyone likes to outdo the next with the great things they're getting to do. Max was all excited about his parents letting him go with his older brother to the Justin Bieber concert on Saturday night. Portia was all about heading to Seattle's Outlet Malls on the weekend, while Jane couldn't stop talking about her dance competition coming up. Mike, of course, brought up the new puppy, and that was my opening to just let out a small tickler that I was going to become a French Bulldog owner any day now. Of course, everyone reacted with disbelief, as they all know my mom and her ability to withstand the pressure I had put on her over the last six months to get my way.

"Get out of here, Ethan," Mike responded. "You aren't ever going to have yourself that little French Bulldoggie. Your mama isn't about to change her mind any time soon for you."

"I know, I know, she isn't going to be happy, but I think I'm about to make it happen without her consent," I replied.

"Oh, Dude, you are going to be in so much doo-doo," Jane taunted. "Your mother is going to disown you over this. How are you going to convince her to let you have it?"

"That's just it, I'm not," I answered. "I plan to earn the cash I need to buy and maintain my dog without her knowing. When she finds out, it'll be too late, and I'll have proven she doesn't have an argument to stand on."

"And just how do you think you're going to manage that one, Ethan? We know you're a talented guy, but come on, be real. How is she *NOT* going to know that you have a new puppy in the house?" Jane asked.

"Stay tuned, my disbelievers, or better yet—join my blog and follow the process online. Pick up my next install-ment tonight—*"Frenchie's Best Friend."* I'm about to astound and impress you all with my exceptional entrepre-neurial skills."

"Well, I say good for you, man—you deserve a dog, if anyone does," Mike replied. "You don't even have a both-ersome brother or sister to harass you; so why shouldn't you get a dog? I think your mom is just plain mean not let-ting you buy one—you've like wanted it *forever!* You let me know if there's anything I can do to help, I'm always in for a little adventure. But remember, when your mom finds out—I didn't know a thing. Not that I'm scared of your mom...MUCH! I really don't want to be on her bad side; she can be pretty excitable!"

"Thanks, Mike—I'll let you know when and if I need you to get involved. And believe me—I know firsthand what you're saying about my mom, but I have this cased. She isn't going to be able to react—except to say, *Welcome to the family, little Frenchie.* I'm going to have the whole thing under control. So no worries! Don't forget, you guys, read my blog tonight."

Once the school day finally ended, I couldn't wait to get over to Grandma Sis' to see what she had in mind and whether we were thinking the same thing. I knew I wouldn't be disappointed—Grandma loves a little "under the radar" action. The only problem with her being a co-conspirator that I could foresee was that she has a bit of a problem with keeping a secret. If she ever let it out (innocently, of course), Mom would "hit the roof" and my life wouldn't be worth living! I think Grandma knows that and she's going to be careful, because she doesn't want to get on the wrong side of Mom, either. She knows my mom can have a temper and isn't pleased when she catches Grandma playing her little games (No doubt it has to do with Dad having some of the same traits…). I'm totally convinced that Grandma is going to be my ideal partner in getting my way.

When I arrived at Grandma's, the "girls" had just finished their bridge game and the party was breaking up. Grandma's friends always make a fuss over me whenever they see me. Now that I'm a teenager, I find it a little embarrassing, but I try to be sociable, as Grandma would think I was rude if I didn't "chat them up" just a bit.

"So Ethan, your grandma tells me there may be a new puppy in your life sometime soon," Mrs. Porter probed.

"Well, Mrs. Porter, I am hopeful I'll have my Frenchie before Christmas, but I have a lot to do before then."

"Ethan, you're such a personable young man, I'm sure whatever you set your mind to do, you can make it happen."

"Thanks, Mrs. Porter—I hope you're right. Time will tell, I guess. So which of you incredible card sharks won the game today?" I asked.

Everyone had a little giggle and they left the house in great spirits. Grandpa was their designated driver, as I think they had had a little glass of afternoon sherry while they played their card game. Finally, Grandma and I were alone, and I couldn't wait to get the plan underway.

"So, Grandma, I saw your face last night while we had dinner with Dad. You were thinking like I was, weren't you? Tell the truth, you know I can make it happen, don't you?" I asked.

"Well, Ethan, I know how badly you want a French Bulldog. It wouldn't be my choice of breed, but I guess that isn't my call. But, yes, I think you're a good boy and you should have your own dog. I disagree with your mom that you aren't responsible enough to take care of a pet. However, that doesn't mean that I want to risk having your mother find out I was involved in helping you go against her wishes. She isn't the most forgiving person I've ever met!" she warned.

"I get that, Grandma, and I think we can do this without her having an inkling that something is going on. When she does figure it out, it will be a done deal and not even Mom could make me give up my puppy, once I have it and have proven that it's all doable, right? You know that, once things have happened, she really doesn't hold a grudge and just accepts it. I think my plan is totally foolproof," I remarked.

"Yes, Ethan, okay, I agree. So let's hear what you think you're going to do."

"Well, Grandma, you heard what's going on with all the dog owners. They don't like to do their own grooming. We have the big laundry tub in the mudroom. I can't see why I couldn't put out flyers in the neighborhood advertising my services between four o'clock and five-thirty each day. It can't be that tricky to wash a dog and blow dry its coat, can it? I'd need some shampoo, a brush, and I guess I could use Mom's blow dryer. She'd never know. Could you supply the shampoo and conditioner from your basement beauty shop? And what about a brush and comb set? You have lots of extras, right?" I asked.

"Okay Ethan, I think you're on the right track," Grandma agreed. "I just wonder if dog owners would put their trust into a thirteen-year-old boy for their dog's care. I mean, you have to realize, Ethan, this is their special pet! How will they know that you aren't going to drown it or wreck their dog's coat? No offense intended, dear."

"None taken, Grandma. I've already thought about that, too. Look, a few of my friends took the babysitting course before we left elementary school. They get babysitting jobs all the time. If I liked little kids better, I could have done that too. What I'm getting at is that, if people will trust their kids with a twelve-year-old, they can be convinced to let *me* groom their dog."

"You know that I have my own clients Ethan. I won't be able to help you groom these dogs. At seventy-two, I still like making money, but it has to be done in between bridge and my stories. I can't be lifting dogs into laundry tubs. I've turned into such a weakling!" she warned.

"Oh no, Grandma Sis, I never expected you to," I replied. "I'm just looking for your advice because you're experienced in business and I need someone to confide in. I may need to ask some small favors along the way, but I'll try not to be too much trouble."

"Ethan, it warms my heart to see my grandson have the determination to work for the thing he wants most. You might just be a 'chip off the old block'! So, how do you propose getting this business underway and how are you going to make sure your mom doesn't find out about it? We'll both be in the 'doghouse' if she does!" she warned emphatically.

"Well, I was thinking last night about how I was going to get clients. I can't have them phoning the house to get bookings, because Mom could answer the phone. I know she usually does her email and computer work at school, so I might be able to get away with online booking through a hotmail address," I suggested.

"Now you're speaking Greek to me. How in the world does that work, Ethan?" Grandma Sis asked.

"It's kind of hard to explain, Grandma, but it's like when you use your cell phone. Sometimes people text message you—so you get a message instantly, but you don't need to speak to them. Since Mom won't let me have my own cell (It's another one of her beefs—kids are bringing them to school, phones are ringing in class, kids are taking inappropriate pictures and posting them on the web, they distract from the learning…), so I'll have to depend upon email through our home computer. It'll work, but the first hurdle is going to be drumming up some customers," I explained to my technically challenged Grandma.

"Well, we know that real doggie spas charge 'an arm and a leg,' so if people pay cash and get a big discount from their usual fee, I think neighborhood dog owners will be happy to give you their business," she replied.

"That's why I thought I'd just hand deliver flyers over the next couple of days and see if anyone bites. Don't you think that, once I have some satisfied customers, they'll spread the word to their friends?" I asked.

"I think so. You just have to get it started and then you'll find that you'll be booked solid. But just between you and me—have you ever even bathed a dog before?" she inquired.

"Actually, no, but I thought you might lend Cher to me today and I would take her home with my supplies and give it a go. That way, I can honestly say in my flyer that I'm a truly experienced groomer," I answered.

"Oh, Ethan, of course you can wash Cher, but you know how fussy Grandpa Bob is about his 'little lady'; he likes her to be totally glamorous at all times! I'll put together your kit of shampoos, conditioners, and brushes, but you'll need to find a good hiding place for all of this, so your mom doesn't notice. And, Ethan, you might want to talk to me about where to keep your earnings once the money starts rolling in…" (Grandma Sis is big on investments and making your money work for you.)

Lots to Learn

I left Grandma Sis' with my arms full of a dog washing kit with Cher in tow, much to her dissatisfaction. She wasn't entirely convinced that she wanted to leave the comfort of her loving home to accompany me around the block with all of those bathing supplies, as she is clever and recognized a "bad sign" when she saw one. Grandma Sis didn't look quite as relaxed with our plan, either, as she did before I told her that I would need to practice my technique on her darling Cher. Funny how that works!

Maybe there was good reason for her to have some misgivings. Let's just say, it wasn't as easy as one may have anticipated. First of all, moving stubborn Cher down the street away from home was a little tricky, since she decided to put the brakes on and I had my hands full. I swear this dog is so spoiled that she actually gets away with temper tantrums. She wouldn't budge. I stopped to get a better grasp of her leash and it fell out of my hand. That little "poof ball" took advantage of the situation and started hightailing it back to Grandma's. I luckily stepped on the leash and stopped her dead in her tracks. Although, dead did go through my mind, as just when I stepped on the leash, she toppled and quit moving momentarily. I held my breath wondering how I would explain her demise to my grandparents. Of course she was just being dramatic and thought she could get her way if she played dead. I was so upset with her, I just yanked on the leash and pulled her all the way back to my house. Man she is one stubborn little dog—I swear she knew what I had in store for her!

I no sooner got her in the door and started to fill the laundry tub with water, than she did a piddle right in the middle of my mom's pristine hardwood kitchen floor. I couldn't believe it—they think kids are defiant—think again! I scooped her up and locked her in the laundry room. Then I frantically used up all the paper towels that were left on the roll to mop up the mess. Of course I needed to hide the evidence of the accident, so I ran the towels out to the trashcan in the garage. As I walked back into the house, I could hear a scratching and splashing sound coming from the laundry room. Do you remember the sound that they used in that old classic thriller, *Jaws,* whenever the shark was about to target another human? That's what came to mind... the "doo-doo, doo-doo, doo-doo" building before he struck his next victim. No lies—when I opened the door, here was Grandma and Grandpa's little darling looking up at me innocently with paint chips attached to her nails and floating in water. How had this happened? I had been gone, what, all of three minutes tops?

I just wanted to plop her right into that overflowing tub of ice cold water, but I grabbed hold of my senses and shouted, "*STAY you little brat!*" while I quickly turned off the laundry tub facet and pulled the plug. Mercifully, the little heathen listened and didn't move a muscle. I don't think anyone had ever spoken to her in that tone before.

Another twenty minutes was spent refilling the tub, mopping up the excess spilled water and wondering how I was going to hide the scratches on the inside of my mom's laundry room door. Oh well, first things first, I had to give Cher her bath. Just as I grabbed for her to put her in the bath, she stopped me cold with a snarl that would have freaked Arnold Schwarzenegger! I'm not kidding you; the lovely precious Cher was actually baring her teeth. I swiftly clamped my hand over her snout and scooped her up with my other hand, landing her immediately in the middle of the tub. Of course, I hadn't really thought about the depth of the water, and she immediately had to revert to dog paddling.

Once again, the plug was pulled to let the water out. The squirming, writhing ball of fur in my hands wasn't about to show me any mercy. She had no intention of letting me calmly administer the shampoo and give her a soothing spa experience. Oh no, she continued to wriggle and thrash, splashing water (yes, I was as completely soaked as the laundry room floor), as I struggled to get a dab of shampoo worked into her coat. I jest when I say "dab." Grandma was great about giving me a liter of her "ladies' shampoo"—only she didn't give me a pump, so when I tried to get a small amount out, it flowed out like a raging river, and dear Cher was completely covered in the shampoo slick. (You've seen the poor ducks covered in oil slick after a spill... it was kind of like that...) I wasn't going to let this little setback deter me. Oh no, I began to massage this quivering mass of slick into Cher's fur. Bewildering as it was to me, the soap appeared to multiply and there were mounds of soapsuds two feet deep. I pulled the plug once again, but the suds didn't seem to dissipate. If anything, it looked like they were multiplying and about to suffocate poor Cher.

I realized that no amount of rinsing was going to get rid of the soapsuds in time, so I whisked Cher out of the laundry tub and ran her through the kitchen and down the hall to the main bathroom. I dropped her into the tub—paying no attention whatsoever to the drips all along my path, and turned on the shower. Of course, in my haste to rescue Cher from bubble suffocation, I forgot to close the shower curtain. Now I had two rooms under water!

Cher was totally indignant by this time—she couldn't believe how obscenely she had been treated! It took all my strength to keep her under the water stream, as she tried to paw her way out of the tub. Finally, I figured she was sufficiently rinsed, so I grabbed my towel off the towel rod and wrapped the poor wet rag into it. Boy did she smell "doggie"—I couldn't help thinking how my towel was going to reek.

Now Grandma had been explicit that Cher with her puffy white hair, must have her coat conditioned. By this time, it was five-thirty, Mom would be home soon and, quite honestly, there was no way I could tackle trying to redo the process in the laundry tub one more time. So, instead, I gave her a good rub down in my towel and the minute I took the towel away she started to race, shake her coat and bark like no one's business. It took me at least ten minutes to corral her in the kitchen and get the leash back on her. By this time, her coat had dried, but it wasn't looking like her usual puff ball hairdo—if you can picture the tufts of hardened, soap-soaked peaks with a flat head. Hmmm, how was I going to get away with this? It occurred to me, ever so gently, that maybe, just maybe, I had a little more to learn about grooming before I sent out those flyers.

With no time to waste, I scurried Cher, the drowned rat, back to Grandma's. I was feverish with worry that mom would walk in on the disaster at home and my plans would be dashed on the *very first day*. Grandma and Grandpa took one look at me and their darling Cher, shook their heads, and made for the salon sink downstairs to rinse their poor dear's coat. Not a word passed their lips other than, "We will talk." (I'm pretty sure my co-conspirator was starting to have second thoughts about the plan, at this point.)

I raced back home and into the kitchen to hear the tail end of a voicemail message where Mom was explaining that she was dealing with a discipline crisis at school and would be about a half hour late. "Thank you, God!" was all I could say.

When Mom showed up totally dazed and done, she couldn't believe that I had soup heating, the whites going in the laundry room (my towel really did stink), and that I had just taken a shower. She was so impressed with my understanding and caring, it made me feel a little guilty that I had, in fact, smeared toothpaste on the laundry room scratches. You would have to wash it or look really closely to know they were there. She didn't suspect a thing and I thought, *"Boy am I good!"*

BLOG of Day 2:

Well, my French Bulldog fans, let me tell you, it's been a day! Although it had a few "ups and downs," I am still confident that I can make this happen. Today was my first experience at washing a dog (thankfully it was Grandma Sis'), and it turned out to be quite a "gong show." I won't give you the gory details, suffice it is to say that Cher (my grandma's Bichon Frisé) returned home in much worse condition than when she was picked up. I may not be quite as equipped to get my Doggie Wash business up and running as quickly as I originally thought. There seems to be an actual technique that one must develop. I think I need to do some research into doggie wash skills before I deliver my flyers. Grandma and I will debrief after school tomorrow, and I think maybe I should try this once again…poor Cher! As for my mother, I was so lucky that she was delayed at work—otherwise she would have caught me in the midst of all the chaos! Tonight I research and tomorrow I continue to develop my grooming skills. I'm still a believer that my Frenchie is going to be mine before long.

Determined and Entrepreneurial,
Frenchie's Best Friend

6

What's the Big Deal?

All that craziness yesterday really took its toll on me; I could barely get myself out of bed. This was probably a good thing as this is more like the real Ethan. My mom would never expect me to be bounding out of bed in anticipation of going to school.

She scared me big time, as she wrinkled her nose during breakfast and asked me if I smelled anything. I quickly denied that there was any kind of smell, but I could tell she wasn't convinced. Of course, it was Cher's dog pee she smelled—I had totally forgot about it and by then the smell had soaked into the hardwood. Oh, if she knew the truth…

My friends were waiting for me when I arrived at school. They had all read the blog and were dying to hear the details of what really occurred. As I entertained them with all of yesterday's insanity, they had lots to say about my antics.

Jane, always a little negative, remarked, "Face it, Ethan, you're beyond help. No one goes into a business not knowing the first thing about it. Who's going to entrust their dog with you? I certainly wouldn't."

"Thanks so much, Jane, for your usual vote of confidence. I'll keep that in mind, as I rake in all those dollars and get my Frenchie," I retorted.

"I think you can do this, Ethan, but I believe you may need BIG MIKE'S support. I obviously know a lot about dogs and dog behavior, having had one since I was a baby. Honestly, man, I think you better lean a little on your friends," Mike suggested.

"Thanks, Mike, I knew you'd get it. Of course you can give me a little help, whenever you have time—you're my man!"

"Well I personally think I'm just going to have a good time reading your blog every night. What could be more entertaining than to have a good laugh over all of your fumbling and mess-ups? Just keep them coming, friend!" Portia mocked.

"I'm so glad that I'm able to keep you amused, Portia, of course that's my main goal," I replied.

Max provoked me with, "Well, Dude, you keep trucking—I say you'll be rolling in dough before long and then it is doggie ownership for you! I've always liked your style, my friend, just dive right in without knowing anything. What's the big deal? Who says those spas hire people with any training anyways?"

"Yeah, Max—thanks for the support; I think. If I can pass French, I can certainly learn how to wash a dog properly. Keep reading my blog—it's only going to get better," I encouraged them.

I was truthfully faking it a bit on the bravado side with my friends—I mean, really, after yesterday, I knew I was going to have to get a lot better at this to make it work. But maybe it's like Max says, it's my style to jump in full-heartedly and then make it work; some people are just made that way. Now, I had to get over to Grandma Sis' house right after school and convince her to let me practice on Cher, yet again. Quite honestly, Cher kind of "freaked me out" yesterday with all of her snarling and craziness, but I'd just breathe deeply and hopefully get through it. Luckily for me, Mom had a staff meeting after school, so she would never make it home before six-thirty. The coast was clear to continue on.

After school, it was directly over to Grandma Sis' for me. When I arrived, Aunt Irene was just getting the finishing touches put on her hairdo in the basement salon. I can be a real schmooze when I need to be.

"Wow, Aunt Irene, don't you look like a "10" with that great do! You'll have to fight off all the guys in your apartment block when they see you walk down the hall." Aunt Irene is what Grandma refers to as an "Old Maid." This means she never got married and doesn't have any kids of her own. Of course, she loves any attention she gets, just like Grandma Sis lives for compliments. (A guy's got to do what a guy's got to do, right?)

"Oh, Ethan, you are such a little smoothie. Speaking of which, are the girls chasing you pretty hard these days at school?" asked Aunt Irene.

"Yeah, it's really tough being such a "chick magnet" like me, Aunt Irene—the girls just never leave me alone!" (wink, wink, nudge, nudge)

"Well, Ethan, just remember, when girls grow up, they look for men with educations and good jobs. You just focus on your schoolwork, and you will never have a problem attracting those girls!" Of course, you guessed it; Aunt Irene is a retired primary teacher. I swear half the family is in education. Where did I come from?

As soon as Aunt Irene left, Grandma Sis came straight to the point. "Okay, Ethan, what exactly did you do to our little Cher yesterday? She's completely traumatized and wouldn't come out of her bed, after we finished rinsing and blow drying her coat. She hasn't been herself all day."

"Well, Grandma, I'm not going to lie to you. I had quite a time with Cher yesterday. She didn't want to cooperate, and my inexperience at grooming was totally obvious to her. However, I think I learned a few things yesterday and know now how to manage her and the bathing more professionally. I obviously really need practice to get more confident with it. Could you see yourself lending me Cher again, today, while Mom's at her staff meeting? It'll give me a chance to try the whole thing once more and put into practice some of the things I messed up on yesterday," I begged.

"As you can see, Ethan, Cher hasn't come out to greet you. I take that as a sign that she hasn't forgiven you for the angst you caused her yesterday. Do you have any idea how you're going to win back her trust? Our little Cher had nightmares after her episode with you yesterday; the poor little puppy was actually howling and whimpering in her sleep!"

"I totally apologize, Grandma, and maybe the first thing I needed to do was to ask you for some pointers about dealing with Cher when you bathe her. I read last night that by getting insight from the dog owners before touching the dog, eases the problems we encountered yesterday. So, what do you say, Grandma, you'll give me some pointers and then let me try bathing her one more time? You will, won't you, Grandma Sis, p-l-e-a-s-e?" I pleaded.

"Okay Ethan, I told you I would help you with this, but I better not have a distressed dog on my hands tonight when she comes back. Grandpa Bob was not pleased, and I had a hard time calming him down after that little fiasco."

"So, tell me what you do to make her more relaxed about having a bath," I said. "Yesterday, I think she smelled my insecurity and then reacted, if what I read last night on the Internet is correct."

Grandma Sis liked being asked her opinion. "We try to make it a game for her. We throw in her favorite squeeze toy into the water and get her excited about going in and getting it. We play a little with her in the water and then we gently and slowly shampoo her with just a *small* dab of shampoo. We never put it near her eyes, but just pull the crud out with our fingers. Then we use the spray to rinse her off, while we let the water run out of the sink. We towel her dry while she's in the sink, so that she doesn't get everything smelling *doggie* wet, and then we let her have a chasing game around the house, while her coat semi dries. She loves tearing around on the carpets. Last of all, we blow dry her coat while we brush it out. She isn't crazy about that, so we feed her treats while we do it. Do you think you can manage?" she asked.

"I have to give this one more try, Grandma, and I'm sure I can. You know me—I can do anything I set my mind to. Now where might I find Cher?"

"That's a good question; I believe she went into hiding the minute she heard you come in…I wonder why!" she chided.

We finally found Cher under the recliner in Grandpa Bob's study, quaking. She looked like a cornered animal when I put the leash on her. Of course, she immediately put her brakes on and whimpered at Grandma. I felt so mean that I was going to have to force her do this once more. However, I had to and that was that. This was business, after all.

I pride myself on being a fast learner, even if my marks at school don't show it. I immediately closed her into the laundry room when we entered my house and went to get all of the things I would need. Of course, I didn't think to ask for some doggie treats, so I poured some chocolate chips into a cup (I mean if kids like chocolate—I'm sure dogs do too, right?). I was smart enough to ask Grandma for the squeezie toy, and I found an old towel in the rag bag, so I figured I was ready to make it happen.

Everything went well, as I started slowly and worked my way into putting her into the bath water with her toy. She was much better behaved, and I only put the smallest dab to shampoo on her coat. Everything was going along smoothly, until I let her loose to air dry her coat. I wasn't thinking and left the laundry room door open. It's like she wanted to get back at me for what I had put her through yesterday. She bee-lined it straight for my mom's bedroom—directly up onto the expensive knit coverlet that she had just recently purchased for her bed. Yep, you guessed it. She decided this was where she was going to run around and air-dry her coat! (I guess the hardwood wasn't cutting it for her.) Unfortunately (for me), her nails had not been clipped lately (Perhaps another skill for me to learn?) and she started to snag the cover in several key spots. Great, just great! How was I going to fix this one? I finally grabbed Grandma's little angel, ready to throttle her, and locked her back in the laundry room. "Just breathe, Ethan, just breathe," I told myself.

Okay, the next new chore was to blow dry her coat. Mom and dad used to play in a bridge club together, so I knew buried in the garage was their old collapsible card table. I found it, cleaned it off and hauled it into the laundry room. Now I had a table to set Cher up on. I set the cup of chocolate chips on the table and then hoisted Cher up. I showed Cher where her treats were and let her get started on nibbling them before I began the process of combing her out. No one could tell me how snarled up her coat would be after a wash. Of course—I had forgotten to put the conditioner on. Cher started snarling again and showing her teeth whenever I pulled on her coat. It seemed to take forever to get the half-dried fur completely dry and snarl free. Did she look her usual puffy fluffy self? No, not entirely. Her coat looked somewhat tired and droopy. (I definitely have some work to do on blow-drying techniques.) At least the chocolate chip cup was completely empty and Cher had enjoyed that part.

So I decided to take her home, and then come back to clean up before Mom would arrive from her meeting. We had just stepped into Grandma and Grandpa's living room and can you believe it—she "tossed her cookies" (Or should I say "tossed her chocolate chips?") on Grandma's prized white carpet. Well, that caused quite a flurry of activity and I chose to vamoose out of there just as quickly as I possibly could to avoid any blame that might be coming my way. It was clear that neither of my grandparents approved of the chocolate chips as an appropriate snack for their Cher!

When I returned home, I had a good look at my Mom's bedding and decided that God was on my side, after all. It actually was almost the same on either side (except for the tag which I handily cut off), and so, when I flipped it over, I figured my Mom would never know.

The rest of the clean up seemed easy, compared to the day before, and I even managed to disinfect the spot on the hardwood where Cher had previously peed. When Mom came home and remarked that the kitchen smelled so clean, I told her I had found something that had dribbled in the garbage and cleaned it up. She did a second take on me—

wondering who this stranger was. I mean, two days in a row I had done some cleaning up; she was incredulous!

BLOG of Day 3

Okay, I admit it—there's somewhat more to this grooming "gig" than I realized. I may have a few more things to sort out before I get my business off the ground. Thankfully, Grandma Sis let me take Cher home with me again for another "go." I don't want to sound like I'm a little full of myself, but I'm feeling a little more in control of the situation tonight (even if chocolate chips aren't the best treat to use as a pacifier, while grooming a dog). Yeah, we had a little "upchucking" issue going on when Cher was returned—of course, she had to wait until she was in the middle of Grandma's white carpet before she let it go…. I'm not sure how Grandma is feeling about her role as my co-conspirator at this point. I think I might lay low tomorrow and do some action research at the Pet Mart out at the strip mall. I need to watch the experts do their work and find out how they charge. That way, I'll figure out how to undercut them to attract my clients. Oh yeah, my friends, I have it all cased. Stay tuned, I'll let you

know what I find out tomorrow after my
sleuthing.

Determined and Entrepreneurial,
Frenchie's Best Friend

Undercover

"Hey Mike, you aren't going to believe this. I have some people following my blog! It's so cool, they're really rooting for me and interested in what I'm doing."

"It was a great idea to blog about it. I need a good laugh every night before going to bed. I can't wait to see what's going to happen when you actually start getting some clients dropping off their dogs. I have this feeling that I'm going to find it all quite hysterical! Hey, do you want me to go with you to Pet Mart after school? I haven't got anything happening and, since I'm a dog owner, it might be helpful…."

"Hey man, you know I'd like that. I'll meet you in front of the gym at three."

Throughout the day, I felt excited about my undercover mission. It was a great feeling to know I was going to have my bud Mike with me. He's actually really knowledgeable about dogs and we make a good team together. People react to me, like I'm a bit of a smart mouth. They see Mike as this real sincere guy; he even passes my mom's criteria for friend material. No doubt he would be able to communicate, better than me, with these groomers.

"Let's go straight to Pet Mart, okay? I have to be home by five. Mom needs me to watch Bobby while she takes Julie to soccer. Are you good with that?" asked Mike. Mike comes from a family of three kids; he is the oldest, and my mom thinks he's a totally responsible guy. She's always pleased when I spend time with him.

We headed straight for the big box store. As we walked in, I couldn't help feeling that this was "doggie heaven" for pet owners. It is the Mecca of "doggie malling." There's every department you can imagine—food, clothing, accessories, toys, bedding, safety, live animals, dog washes, grooming, etc. You name it, Pet Mart has it. What it doesn't have (and I picked up on this immediately) is a personal touch. It's like this one boutique where my mom buys all of her clothes. She doesn't care (like Grandma Sis does) that the clothes are more expensive. She feels she gets personalized attention when she goes in there to shop. The associates know her by name, they know what styles she loves, and she never feels ignored or overly pestered. She's loyal to her boutique because of the service. Pet Mart missed that little secret to success—I could tell. We headed straight for the Dog Grooming area.

The first thing that struck us was *THE SIGN*.

Absolutely no pet owner is allowed beyond this point!

My first reaction was, "Now that's real friendly!" I took a deep breath—I wasn't sure these guys were going to be open and ready to share their knowledge with a couple of kids.

We walked up to the counter, where you drop off your dogs, just as a groomer came out from the back area; probably where the tubs were.

Mike got his attention as he was going by. "Hey, man, have you got a minute?"

The groomer stopped and approached us from his side of the counter. "Is there something I can help you guys with?" he asked.

"Yea, I have a Golden Retriever and we're thinking of bringing her in to be groomed. I'd like some information about what kind of service Pet Mart provides and, of course, the fees you charge," Mike explained.

"Well, I can give you this brochure, it outlines it pretty much for you," answered the groomer.

"So what kind of qualifications do you have to have at Pet Mart to become a groomer?" I interjected.

"Well, there are two levels in the grooming department. Some do the bathing and others do the grooming. The bathers learn on site, while the groomers take a course." he answered.

"My dog is pretty big. Do you have any problem with grooming the larger breeds?"

"No, not at all, we take them big or small, and they get the grooming you ask for."

"Do you ever have any problems with certain dogs? I mean you must have some that are hard to handle like a Pit Bull or something. Can their owners come in the back and help soothe them during the bath?" I asked. (I really wanted to know how they would control a dog like that!)

"Naw, we can't have anyone in the back except employees. There's often water on the floor and other things that could cause an accident. Let's face it—Pet Mart wouldn't want to be liable for an accident, now would we? Hey, I'd like to talk to you guys more, but I have a Shih Tzu waiting for me in the back, and she is one impatient little dog. Just read the brochure; it'll give you all the info you need. Bring your retriever in—we'll give him a good wash."

"Well, that wasn't really helpful was it? You didn't find out any of their grooming tricks from that guy," said Mike. "I bet there's a lot of crazy stuff happening back there that they don't want the customers knowing about and that's the real reason the pet owners can't cross the line."

"You're probably right, but at least I have their price list—so I know what the competition is charging. Let's just walk through the supplies and see if there's anything I should be buying. I have the shampoo, conditioner, and brushes already and, of course, *no* money."

"Ethan, you're going to need nail clippers—you do know that, right?"

"You think they really want me touching their dog's nails? I don't know about doing that…. Let's check them out." When we got to the clipper aisle, my reaction was, "Are you kidding me? They cost a fortune—I think I'll see how my human clippers work first. There's no way I can buy these now."

"Okay, Ethan, but I have a feeling human clippers aren't exactly the right tool for dogs, but you'll see…I have to run, I've got ten minutes to make it home in time. Catch you later, bro."

As Mike left, I decided to look through some of the pet care books on their shelves. Unbelievable, there were piles of books written on the subject. How could these authors come up with so many different grooming topics to write about? I'm not a real bookworm or anything, but I don't mind books that have a lot of pictures. These grooming books were kind of interesting. I just happened to flip to the section on "Trimming Your Dog's Nails." There were pages and pages—it made it look way too complicated. I mean really, what's the big deal? You cut the nail with clippers or your mom's manicure scissors and presto, the job is done. Why bother writing page after page on the technique? What a waste of time! I closed the books and returned them to their shelves. It was time to head for home myself. Mom would be home soon, and I didn't want to have to lie to her about where I was after school.

BLOG of Day 4

Well, my fellow bloggers, it was a pretty uneventful day without any "hands on" practice, but my friend Mike and I tried to get information out of a groomer at the Pet Mart. He wasn't sharing any tricks or techniques, but we scored their price list and brochure of their services. I've worked up a flyer that shows the price slashing I'm doing in comparison with what they offer. The plan is to print these off tomorrow after school (when Mom won't know that I'm using up her printer ink) and then deliver them to all the homes in our neighborhood that I know have dogs. Hopefully, I'll be getting some bookings real soon. I'm ready for the challenge because I know my baby Frenchie is coming to live with me just as soon as I make enough money. It's only a matter of time…I can do this.

Determined and Entrepreneurial,
Frenchie's Best Friend

8

Here Come the Customers—
Ready or Not

I raced home after school the next day to get the flyer finished and printed off. This is what it ended up looking like.

NEIGHBORHOOD DOG WASH

Are you sick of the high costs charged by **BIG BOX PET STORES** and over-priced **DOGGIE SPAS?** Well then, read on, you clever pet owners, because I have a deal for you!

A **DOG GROOMING BUSINESS** has opened up in your neighborhood. That's right; practically in your backyard! If you are looking for a dog wash and don't want to pay the high costs of the exclusive spas, enjoy the convenience that Ethan will deliver right in your own part of town.

To book your next dog wash appointment, just email GetFrenchie@hotmail.com. Remember, bookings are **4:00–5:30, Mondays to Fridays.** This means that only a few, select customers will be able to access this exclusive offer.

Enjoy the convenience of having your dog groomed, right in your neighborhood at a fraction of the regular fee.

Bath with Conditioner $20.00

Bath with Conditioner and a Blow Dry $25.00

Book your appointment today!

I thought that if I didn't mention nails, I would be off the hook. The flyer pretty much said it all, and if I could get the business started, I was sure that everything would fall into place. I knew Mom had a stash of neon lime paper that I figured she wouldn't miss, so I helped myself to it. I ran off the entire stack just as the printer predictably sent a message saying the colors were out of ink. I could count on having to answer to my mom on that one; she's super strict about printing in colors, ever since she realized that the refills are more expensive than the entire printer! By then I knew I had about an hour left to get on my bike and start delivering these babies to the pet owners looking for convenience and savings.

Right around our house, I was careful to go to only the houses I knew my mom didn't know the people and therefore wouldn't have a talk with them about my business. I tried to put the flyers in the houses where there was evidence of a dog presence. I had a close call, where a Guard Dog wasn't too friendly—thinking I was a mailman and just about attached his jaws to my leg. Lucky for me, I got away with just a little of my pant leg unraveling, as I sped down the street on my bike. Their house definitely did *not* get my flyer! I stopped at Grandma Sis' and covertly handed her a flyer. Grandpa Bob was busy weeding and hardly looked up as I tore into their house.

"Well, my boy, it looks like you're on your way to getting your French Bulldog, after all. I think the flyer looks great! But have you noticed that the minute Cher saw you open the door, she high-tailed it out of here? She's out there quaking beside Grandpa, hoping you won't come near her. I think she's still traumatized by the practices earlier in the week. I hope your new customers won't have the same reaction! Are you completely set up, and have you thought it through so that your mom is *NOT* going to catch on to what is happening in her laundry room?"

"Yeah, I think I'm good, Grandma. The people who come to me are going to be looking for a bargain. I'm hoping they won't want to have nails trimmed, as I don't have the clippers and, quite honestly, I read about how to do it on the Internet and it freaked me out a little. It's kind of tricky to do it without hurting the dog, I think."

"Well, I guess we'll see what happens…remember, the fewer dollars you have to spend, the more cash in your pocket to put towards your puppy."

"Okay, Grandma, I'm heading home and see whether I have any bookings online yet. I'm getting pretty excited about this. Who knew I would love going into business?!"

When Mom walked in, I had just finished checking my emails. I had a booking for the next day—I couldn't believe it. I felt like bouncing off the walls, as I knew things were getting underway and I had a foolproof plan. Mom wanted to know why I was on the computer, and I quickly covered myself with a story about research for a class project on ancient civilizations. She bought it and said she would see what she could dig up for me in her resources at school, as well. I knew she was just too fatigued to worry about my schoolwork, and we started to get dinner underway. We actually make a pretty good team, as we like to cook together and, sometimes, Mom even remembers to take something out in the morning to defrost.

After dinner, Mom relaxed in the den watching her therapeutic *Law and Order* reruns, while I got back online to double check the bookings. I couldn't believe it—there were three more customers setting up appointments. Of course, some people didn't read the flyer completely and thought they could book on Saturdays—I DON'T THINK SO! Man, I really had to get myself organized and make sure that I wasn't overbooking. I always knew there was a purpose for my school agenda! So, after emailing back and forth, I thought I had it all figured out and scheduled well. Hopefully I was right.

BLOG of Day 5

I will have to be brief tonight. Mom is just finishing her show and will be checking up on me before long. Things have suddenly gotten super busy. That's right, my Frenchie admirers, out in Blog World, the flyers are delivered and I have four bookings already. My first customer will show up tomorrow after school. This is perfect, as Mom has a staff party to go to and that means she definitely won't show up before I finish with my first customer. I'm so excited, I'll have my first $25 saved toward my puppy by this time tomorrow night—YIPPEE!!! Wish me luck, fellow bloggers—I really appreciate your online encouragement.

Determined and Entrepreneurial,
Frenchie's Best Friend

9

My First Appointment

I felt like the entire day dragged on forever. Would I ever get home to set up for my first appointment? Finally, the dismissal bell rang, and I bolted for the door. Mike stepped in front of me in the corridor, as I was bounding towards the exit door.

"Hey, man, I haven't seen you all day. Is everything okay? I guess you can't stay and shoot some baskets tonight in the sports court, not with your BIG APPOINTMENT looming."

"Yeah, Mike, no time to waste. I have to get home so I'm ready when they drop off their dog. Hopefully, this first one will be cool—wish me luck. Read my blog tonight. I'll update it with all the gory details," I called over my shoulder as I ducked past him.

As I raced home to meet my first client, I was doing a mental checklist of what I needed to do to prepare for "Tiny" (that was the dog's name on the email). I was visualizing one of those cute little Yorkshire Terriers that my mom always refers to as little "rat dogs." I felt kind of guilty to charge them $25 for such a teeny, little dog, but business is business.

Luckily, I made it home in record time and got everything set up in the laundry room. I decided to set out a bowl of goldfish crackers (instead of chocolate chips), in case I needed to bribe the little guy to stand still while I blow-dried his coat. Just as I turned off the water facet, the doorbell rang.

I opened the door to see a tiny woman trying to hold onto the biggest, dirtiest English Sheepdog I had ever laid my eyes on. She held on for dear life to the leash, as she tried to get "Tiny" under control.

"Excuse me, do I have the right spa? I'm looking for Ethan, The Discount Dog Groomer. Am I at the right address? I didn't see any business sign," the woman said. At this point, the very large, very straggly Sheepdog was straining to dash through the door.

I gulped and replied, "You do have the right address and I am Ethan. So... this is *Tiny*. His name really fits! I have Tiny booked for a wash, conditioner, and a blow dry. He has a pretty long coat, so I think it's safe to say that you won't need to pick him up any time before five-thirty."

"Well, I can see you're a little surprised to meet Tiny—his name is a little deceiving. Most groomers are somewhat astonished when I come in for our first grooming," she replied.

I just bet they are, lady, I thought. *How in the world am I going to get this dog done in an hour and a half?* I wondered.

"I have to say, you're a bit of a shock to me, as well," remarked Tiny's owner. "I was expecting someone a little more mature and experienced. Are you sure you know how to do this? Tiny was up at the lake house this week, and he has a lot of burrs and things caught in his fur. He isn't real keen about having his coat brushed out, so he can be quite a handful."

"Oh, I don't want you worrying about a thing," I replied with as much bluster as I could muster. "I'm going to have him looking just perfect by the time you pick him up. Please do make sure you are here by five-thirty for pick-up, won't you?"

"Alright then, Ethan, I'll pass the leash over to you, and Tiny is in your capable hands. I'll be back by five-thirty. You be a good boy Tiny, don't you give Ethan any trouble, no you be mama's good boy and be nice and clean when I pick you up," she gushed.

As I closed the door behind Tiny's owner, I had to grab hold of the leash in both hands and struggle to move him in the direction of the laundry room—I have no idea how a 50 kg thirteen-year-old was able to drag a 100 kg Sheepdog anywhere! Of course, once I got Tiny into the laundry room, I had no idea how I was going to get this "beast" into the bathwater. I may not be the top student in my school, but I can be resourceful, thankfully! I went out to the garage and hauled in the folding table and the old kitchen chair that Mom keeps around for a garage sale that never happens. I set it up so that by pushing Tiny from the behind, I got him up on the chair; from there, more pushing had him moved onto the table. What I didn't expect was a dog who loves water. That's right; in one massive leap, the gargantuan did a belly flop off of the table top into the tub of water. Tidal wave!! Water splashed all over the walls and the floor, and Tiny looked at me like, "Where did the water go?" So, of course, more water was needed to go into the tub, but hard to do with Tiny deciding it was playtime. Alright, I admit it, by that point, I was already exhausted and panting like a dog, but there was no way that I could give up; I had this gigantic brute to get washed, dried, and combed out—all within an hour. "Please God, give me a little help here!" I silently prayed.

Once I started scrubbing, I realized that I was going to really need to rinse him thoroughly; there wasn't going to be any shortcut to getting the soap and conditioner out. And Tiny's owner wasn't kidding when she said he was a mess; the mats were huge and full of all kinds of foreign materials. I just went into panic mode, and I scrubbed Tiny like there was no tomorrow. I don't think I have ever worked as feverishly in my life! It took three tubfuls to rinse this dog, and I don't want to tell you about all of the guck that went down my Mom's laundry tub drain… It was truly scary!

Now I was working against the clock. I had to get this dog out of the tub, onto the table and get him dried and combed out. It was one thing to aid the "big lug" into the tub, but how to entice him out? Who knew some dogs actually love water and baths? Then I remembered the cheddar fish crackers, hoping this dog likes food more than baths. I set up a trail across the table and can you believe it? The crazy mutt went for the crackers—YES! So now I had him on the table, but how was I going to keep him up there? I remembered the abandoned leash and tied him tightly so that he couldn't jump off. He was okay at this point, but I realized this was only going to hold him as long as he was okay with being up there. GOLDFISH CRACKERS—I NEEDED TO KEEP FEEDING THE BEAST.

No one could have told me that this was going to be so difficult. I didn't realize how hard it is to dry a dog this size in a wet, smelly, little room. Five towels—that's what it took to towel dry him. And then the fun began. As I tried combing out his tangles, simultaneously feeding him and trying to balance my mom's blow dryer, let me tell you, it was no small feat. It left me with ten minutes before his owner would be picking him up, and I only had him about half done. I decided to concentrate on the tangles, as I figured that would be the part she would want done the most. I'll say one thing for Tiny—as long as his tummy was being fed, he could have cared less about the tangles. Grandma's brush wasn't much help, the bristles were falling out and getting caught in the tangles. My fingers were doing a better job of it. I worked like a crazed maniac and thankfully didn't run out of the crackers (the entire Costco-sized box, I might add) until I was almost done. The doorbell rang just as the cracker supply ran out. I didn't have to worry about how I was going to get Tiny off of the table. The doorbell set him off and he jumped to the floor with the table and leash attached. Getting the leash under control took a little maneuvering, but with luck, I got it out from under him and the table leg and made my way to the door.

As I opened the door, I heard, "Well there's my *'teeny Tiny.'* I hope you were a good boy for Ethan and let him get you nice and clean."

And then to me she said, "Ethan, I am so impressed. You actually got most of the mats out in record time. Whenever I take him to our usual doggie spa after we've been up at the lake house, they get really cranky and pout about the amount of work they had to do. I think you did a great job. I'll definitely want to bring Tiny back after our next weekend trip. But before we go, can you tell me what that orange substance is around his snout? I've never seen that on his fur before."

"Oh not to worry, it's a special powder I have for helping get rid of the discoloration around his mouth from his dog food. It should disappear in the next day or so and take the discoloration with it." (Who says I can't think on my feet?)

"Well, Ethan, say good-bye to Tiny and we will be back—oh I almost forgot—here is your $25 fee and I have an extra $10 for taking such good care of my "Teeny Tiny.""

I shut the door and collapsed on the floor thinking, *I may never get up off this carpet for the next two days. I'm sure I can't move!* At that very moment, the phone rang, and I could hear my mom saying into the answering machine to her latchkey kid, "Ethan, I'm on my way home. I'm just going to stop and pick us up a pizza and movie, so don't start anything."

You never saw anyone move so fast in your life. I was off that floor in a split second. The walls and floor of the laundry room were mopped up, the towels were in the wash, I returned everything to the garage, and then I got out one of Mom's scented candles from her bathroom and lit it.

No sooner had I blown the candle out again and returned it to her bathroom, her headlights shone into the house, as she pulled into the driveway.

Mom doesn't miss much, especially on a Friday night, when she is excited about having a free night ahead of her. She was all thrilled about finding not one, but two decent movies for us to "vedge" with in front of the TV. As she was getting the pizza out on plates, she made a face and remarked, "Ethan, what do I smell? I'd swear it smells like wet dog in here!"

I countered quickly with, "You know, I took the short-cut home tonight and I think as I walked through the long grass I got a whiff of doggie scent on my jeans. That's why the laundry is going, I put my clothes in the washer. Anyways, just take a deep breath of this yummy pizza—I can't wait to dig in."

Mom had to wake me up after the second movie. Apparently, I had fallen asleep exactly ten minutes into the first one. (Little did she know what kind of a week I had put in, but I fell asleep with a smile on my face—there was thirty-five dollars tucked away in my wallet....)

Blog of Day 6

All right all of you naysayers who thought it couldn't be done...*I did it, I did it!* I had my first customer yesterday and she was so pleased with my work that she tipped me $10. That's right—I'm $35 richer than I was the day before, and that is just my first step towards becoming a French Bulldog owner. I can already picture my perfect little bulldog. He's going to be mostly black with copper-colored brindling, and his little pug face is going to be so cute, no one will be able to resist his kisses. When I walk him at the doggie park, all the other dog owners are going to be jealous that I have the coolest dog there. I can just visualize us doing everything together; he's going to be my shadow. It will be worth the pain of doing business. Okay, I admit it, it was quite an ordeal yesterday and I was so wiped out afterwards, I couldn't stay awake long enough to even blog you about it. Let me just say, *do not ever anticipate the breed of the dog based on its name.* "Tiny" wasn't what I expected: a dirty, matted English Sheepdog is what I washed. Now visualize all of that happening in our very small laundry room. You get the picture. I'm still amused by the fact that her dog had goldfish cracker stains around his mouth. (It was how I bribed the dog while I attacked his mats, okay?) When she picked him up, I told her it was a special powder to take out the food stains from her dog's fur and, get this…she bought it! I am booked solid—all five days next week. Can you believe it? I may have enough saved BEFORE Christmas at this rate. Keep the faith everyone.

Determined and Entrepreneurial,
Frenchie's Best Friend

10

Business Flourishes

Who would have thought that so many people are looking for a bargain that they would book their dog's grooming with me? I couldn't believe the number of bookings I had. The entire month was almost completely scheduled and, at this rate, I wasn't going to have any trouble meeting my goal. However, I had to admit all of this "espionage entre-preneuring" had had a few close calls and there were times when I was certain that my mom was going to figure it all out. I didn't even want to visualize what that would look like.

For example, she started to notice that the towels were always getting washed. I had to convince her that I was going through an obsessive-compulsive disorder stage where I couldn't use a towel twice for any reason; that's why I was using the older towels, so I wouldn't wear out her newer ones. I knew all about this disorder because Mom had had a student a couple of years ago that was really obsessive-compulsive. He was constantly washing his hands and wouldn't touch doorknobs or even his desktop. It was quite a trial for my mom to normalize his behavior to the other students in her class and she used to talk about it a lot at home. I had to really play it up that I was fighting the disorder, but something in me just made me have to have a different towel every time I washed—even my hands. How I pulled that one off, I'll never know. She was super skeptical, but finally just gave in to it. My persuasive language skills were improving, no doubt about it! Or Mom was just too fatigued to figure out what was really happening under her roof.

She also noticed the amount of printer ink that I went through when I ran off the flyers. She was furious when she went to run off special certificates for her class and all she could access was the black ink. I blamed it on my Socials teacher, saying she wouldn't accept our project unless it was run off in color. I explained that it was my responsibility to print the entire project for my group with pictures and Power Point slides. She was ready to call the school and complain about their policy, saying it was time for them to join the 21st century and stop wasting paper and ink and that high school kids should be able to forward their projects to their teacher digitally. I calmed her down by saying my history teacher was really struggling technologically and that she had admitted she just couldn't cope with all the new demands on her time and expertise that keeping up with technology was causing. Mom wasn't that sympathetic, as she expects every educator to be like her—dedicated to keeping up with innovative practices, including technology. I begged her not to complain this time and she finally agreed. Boy was I relieved, that one was a close call.

And then there was the Draino conversation. That's right, she went to hand wash some of her delicates and found that the sink in the laundry room wasn't draining properly. She poured the Draino down and it seemed to do the trick, but she just couldn't understand how the sink that rarely was used would become clogged. Go figure...

Monday's Appointment

You have to understand that, although I had been reading up on dog grooming techniques on the Internet whenever I had a chance, I really was limited in the time I could spend on this. When I welcomed my second appointment in, the man who brought in his Schnauzer cautioned me about not forgetting that Fritz (the dog's name) was going to need a thorough teeth brushing.

Are you kidding me, man? Where on my flyer did it say that I brush your dog's teeth? I thought. But in reality, I assured Mr. Schultz that he could count on a minty fresh, gleaming-white dog smile when he picked up Fritz.

Oh sure, Ethan, how are you going to pull this one off? I questioned myself, silently.

As soon as Mr. Shultz had departed, I got Fritz right into the bath water. He had kind of a crabby disposition, that dog. Let's just say that soaping him up around his face and mouth area was a challenge. The little brute actually wanted to nip and snarl at me, and I was supposed to *brush his teeth?*

Well, I knew I wasn't going to sacrifice my toothbrush to Fritz and I didn't think using my Mom's electric Braun was going to cut it. So what was my alternative? This dog wasn't going to let me anywhere near his teeth. His crotchety attitude was actually pretty unnerving. He kind of scared me, if you really want the truth. So what to do?

I had the perfect solution! Everyone has watched the commercial where the woman has eaten lunch at work and she needs to floss her teeth, so she tries scotch tape. That doesn't work, to get that fresh clean feeling one gets from brushing and flossing, so she pops in a piece of Extra Professional Gum with micro granules. Guess who just happened to talk his mom into buying a case of that particular gum at Costco on the weekend? That's right my friends.

I took Fritz out of the tub and got him dried and brushed and then I opened a pack of Extra. I felt like a genius as he chomped into the first piece. Unfortunately he gave it a couple of chews and it disappeared. Yep, he swallowed it. Well, obviously, one little chew wasn't going to satisfy his owner, and he still didn't have that great minty smell that indicates his breath was better from the cleaning. *So… what other choice did I have?* I had to open the rest of the packet and feed them to him one at a time. I figured he was averaging about two chews to each piece. By the time the package had been devoured, I was sure his teeth looked whiter and his breath certainly was a far cry from the stench it had been before I fed him the gum.

When Mr. Schultz picked Fritz up, the first thing he did was lean close to Fritz's face and give him a sniff. I held my breath, worried that he would realize that I had not really brushed Fritz's teeth.

"Well, Ethan, I can see that you have a way with these animals. Fritz doesn't usually like having his teeth brushed, but you obviously have some technique that works for him. His breath smells just like spearmint, what a great job you did, my boy."

I thought, *You just wait until Fritz poops out that wad of gum that's moving through his digestive system; you might not be so impressed.* Boy, I sure hoped he wouldn't develop some sort of constipation issue because I fed him all of that gum…

Instead, I replied, "Thanks, Mr. Schultz, I'm glad you're satisfied. Of course, I will have to charge you an extra five dollars for the added service."

"I'm happy to pay that for such good service, Ethan," Mr. Shultz replied, "and here's an extra five dollars to show my appreciation."

Well how about that?....I trust Fritz's dental treatment didn't end up costing Mr. Shultz a massive vet bill for an inability to digest the package of gum sitting in his dog's gut!

Blog of Day 7

I am completely impressed with myself today. Through taking on this dog grooming business, I have found out something about myself. I can think fast on my feet—I'm not sure another thirteen-year-old would have come up with the same solution to brushing a dog's teeth, as I did today. That's right, dear readers, my customers continue to challenge me. I didn't include teeth brushing on my flyer, but they just assume that if they want a service, I can provide it. When little Fritz (my Schnauzer customer) left, I looked up the correct procedure for brushing a dog's teeth and learned that groomers use a plastic sock over their 2 fingers that has special bristles on it and a paste. I felt rather smug after reading this, as my technique may not have been the most conventional approach (or healthy), but I did get the required result. When Fritz left my shop, he had the freshest smelling mouth in the neighborhood and the whitening factor of the pack of Extra that he consumed had considerably brightened his previously foul looking teeth. Now you may be thinking this was not an entirely wise solution, but you didn't face Fritz. There was no way that cranky little beast was going to let me into his mouth with a brush and toothpaste, but when I fed him gum, he loved it. I just hope that he is discreet in passing the gum and that Mr. Shultz never discovers my tooth-brushing technique! Another exciting day tomorrow, I have a sweet Cocker Spaniel coming my way.

I've been searching the Internet for French Bulldog breeders, and it looks like my puppy will cost somewhere in the neighborhood of seventeen hundred dollars and up to three thousand! Yikes, that's going to take a lot of dog washing! I have a ways to go, but I can do it. You just watch it all unfold, my fellow bloggers. And thanks for your input and encouragement—I have to say your comments are inspirational to this thirteen-year-old "dog groomer!" I'm smart enough to recognize that I need all the help that I can get!

French Bulldog Fund: **Day One** **$35.00**
Day Two **$35.00**
TOTAL: **$70.00**

Determined and Entrepreneurial,
Frenchie's Best Friend

Tuesday's Appointment

The doorbell rang and I was totally organized and all set up for my next client. A woman with long flowing hair entered with her beautiful Cocker Spaniel. Her dog already looked like she was "groomed to the nines," complete with a purple bow holding up her bangs identical to her owner's. My first thought was, *How can I possibly make this dog look better groomed than she already is?* I had my answer almost immediately.

"Hi, Ethan, this is Sugar and she truly is a little sweetheart. I like to keep her really well groomed and maintaining her beautiful shiny coat is a priority for me. The problem is that she is allergic to many of the shampoos I have tried at home, so that's why I bring her in to the Doggie Spas for her baths, as they have the proper hypo allergenic products that will ensure she doesn't get itchy and have the sneezes. You do have the special soaps for dogs with her type of issue, don't you, Ethan?" she asked.

"Yes, of course, Mrs. White, I am well equipped to deal with all allergic issues of my clients, I can assure you!" I lied.

As I spoke, I simultaneously thought, *She's got to be kidding me! How in the world would I have a clue what to use on a dog with allergies…oh…this is going to be bad—I feel it in my gut!*

The minute she walked out the door, I hauled Sugar over to the phone in the kitchen and dialed Grandma Sis. Luckily she answered, as she and Grandpa Bob were just watching the end of Oprah. I could tell she was distracted, as she doesn't like anyone to interrupt them when they are watching their shows. I apologized profusely and gave her the scoop on my latest dilemma.

"Grandma, I'm in trouble here. I have a Cocker Spaniel that has serious allergies and needs a special soap, or else she gets itchy all over and sneezes. I assured the owner that I had the right products to wash her dog, but you and I both know I don't. What can I do? You're a hairdresser. Is there anything you know about hypo allergenic shampoos?"

"I'm sorry, Ethan, did you say you are feeling a little overly hyper about shampooing a Cocker Spaniel? Just a moment, Ethan, I have to see what Oprah is gifting to her studio audience; it's just too exciting…Oh my, everyone goes home with their own IPad—whatever that is!"

"Grandma, I'm sorry to bug you, but I really need your help here! The clock is ticking and I have to get this dog done before Mom gets home." I couldn't keep the panic out of my voice.

"Okay, Ethan, you have my attention. So what's going on? Just a minute, I'm going to go in the kitchen so Grandpa can watch the news."

"Grandma, I have a Cocker Spaniel that is super allergic to regular shampoos. Her owner says that if she isn't bathed with the right products, she itches and sneezes. What am I going to do? Do you have any of this special kind of hypo allergenic shampoo?"

"You know, Ethan, I really don't. I've always thought all this allergy stuff is just a figment of everyone's imagination—including your mom's. That's right, Ethan, she uses hypo allergenic cosmetics from Clinique. I would bet money that if you look in her shower, you'll find the shampoo she uses is just that. Let me know how it works out, Ethan. I'm sure the dog will be fine. I better get back to the living room or Grandpa will be suspicious that we're up to no good."

I raced with Sugar in tow to my mom's bathroom. Sure enough, there was a half empty bottle of Clinique shampoo in her shower, and it said it was hypo allergenic! "Thank you, God—I knew you were looking out for me," I acknowledged.

When Mrs. White arrived to pick up her sensitive Sugar, she was thrilled to see her pet's lovely, shiny coat and her dog calmly sitting by the door without any visible signs of itchiness or wheezing.

"Ethan, I'm very impressed with your work. Sugar seems so calm and content after her bath; you obviously used a top of the line hypo allergenic product on her. I want to tip you for the extra precaution that you took for my Sugar. There's a ten dollar tip and your service is still a much better deal than the regular doggie spas. Thanks, Ethan. Sugar will be returning to you."

I hope not too often, Mrs. White, I thought. That shampoo I used from my mom's shower had the price tag on the bottom of the bottle and let's just say that the ten dollar tip wasn't going to pay half of the costs for a replacement bottle. I sure hoped Mom didn't notice that a significant amount of her expensive shampoo was missing.

Blog of Day 8

Well, my fellow blog readers, who knew that dogs have allergies, just like people? Not me, that's for sure! So the challenge today was to bathe the sweetest Cocker Spaniel who just happens to get itchy and sneezes if she isn't bathed with hypo allergenic products. What do I know about allergies and products used to prevent the symptoms? Absolutely nothing! Thankfully for my lifeline (Grandma Sis), she had the perfect solution. Unbeknownst to me, my mom suffers from allergies (I knew that) and she has to use special cosmetics and products to cause her less aggravation (I didn't know that, why would I?). Lucky for me, Grandma Sis did know and sure enough, Mom had Clinique shampoo in her shower and it did the trick. Sugar was bathed, content, and looking beautiful for her owner when she was picked up, and there wasn't a sign of an issue. Once again, my customer left satisfied and inclined to leave me a tip. I've decided that since these clients are so used to the regular exorbitant prices of the spas, they feel like they should tip because of the great deal they believe they're getting. Anyways, it just seems that every customer I have had so far has

ended up paying me thirty-five dollars—
I'm not complaining.

   Who knows what tomorrow will bring?
I'll keep you posted. Have I told you
how awed I am by the number of bloggers following my journey? You are the
best—it helps me feel less isolated
as I work towards my goal. And guess
who cleared their first hundred dollars? I'm ecstatic and Grandma Sis is
already trying to come up with more
services we can add to increase the
bottom line—you gotta love her! She'll
be investing my profits in the Stock
Market before I know it!

French Bulldog Fund: Day One   **$35.00**
                    Day Two   **$35.00**
                    Day Three **$35.00**
TOTAL: **$105.00**

Determined and Entrepreneurial,
Frenchie's Best Friend

12

Wednesday's Appointment

When I woke up this morning, I was completely relaxed as I anticipated the little Pug coming over after school. I have a soft spot for this breed, as they somewhat remind me of my favorite—the French Bulldog. I figured this one would be "a walk in the park." Who knew?

When I arrived at school that morning, Mike was waiting for me. We hadn't had much time these days to "just hang" a little together after class with all my scheduled appointments. Anyways, he wanted to come home with me and help with my Pug after school. I couldn't see why not, so we agreed to meet up after our last class and he would be my assistant with this client.

"Mike, I just have to set up the laundry room for the appointment. Go and find a snack while you wait on me," I directed him.

Mike is my best friend and he's quite at home at our place and fine with scrounging up an after-school snack on his own. Mike passes my mom's inspection; she thinks he comes from a good family, and she trusts that when we're at home together, without her supervision, we can be counted upon to make good choices for how we spend our time. I think she might have second thoughts if she knew about the doggie grooming business, but these are extraordinary times, right?

When the doorbell rang, I met Max, the Pug, and Mr. Grant. Max was truly a cutie, and I took to him right from the get-go. That is, right up until Mr. Grant let me know his expectations for the grooming of Max.

"Ethan, as you know from being a dog groomer, some dogs have to have their anal glands cleaned. Poor Max has been dragging his butt on the carpet for the last couple of days, and Mrs. Grant is fed up with that, I can tell you. So please do make sure that you clean them out, so he is fresh to take home. I don't want any more matrimonial strife over Max's overflowing glands. Thanks son."

"I'll be right on that, Mr. Grant, yep you can count on me!" I assured my customer. Mike and I exchanged distressed looks, as Mr. Grant walked out the door.

"Ethan, what have you done? You don't know anything about expressing anal glands—I know you don't. And I only know the correct terminology because my cousin's dog had an issue with his dog's anal glands, and they had to get the vet to do it for them. This is really gross; I can't believe you got us into this," Mike whined.

"Okay, Mike, get hold of yourself. Let's think this through. I had to agree because these clients all think that I have had training. If I say I can't do what they request, they won't leave their dog with me and word will get out that I don't have a clue what I'm doing, and I'll NEVER get to have my Frenchie! So let's figure this out. Do you have your laptop with you today?"

"Yeah, I've got it. What are you suggesting, we Google 'anal gland cleaning'?" he asked.

"That is precisely what I'm suggesting, my friend. Get it fired up, while I start bathing this cute mutt."

"Okay, Ethan, all I can say is that it makes me want to throw up just reading this, let alone watching the video. You are going to have to do it by yourself, I really have a weak stomach, and this is too gross, seriously, man! And Ethan, I think you better consider wearing rubber gloves; it's going to be nasty."

"Alright, Mike, get my mom's rubber gloves from under the kitchen sink and then slowly read me the technique. I can do this...I think."

"Okay, Ethan, here we go my friend; this is a dirty dog business. I really think Max's owner should take him to a vet to have this done; it's complicated and repulsive!"

"Mike, I need you to be strong for me, okay, buddy? Just read it slowly, and I'll manage the rest, trust me!"

"Okay, Ethan, here goes nothing...Hold Max's head to the left and his butt to the right. Now, lift Max's tail upwards firmly in your left hand. *Oh puke, look at that mess around his butt hole, I'm going to throw up, I swear. I'm getting the dry heaves!*"

"Mike, stay focused. I need you to read the instructions; I'm the one that has to do the dirty work. Now what am I supposed to do? Max isn't going to let me keep him in this position for very long."

"It's up to you, Ethan; it's your problem. Here we go. Press on both sides of the dog's anus using your thumb and your index finger with your right hand."

"*Oh yuck, really! I seriously have to go in there?*" I couldn't believe it!

"That's what it says. I can't look, Ethan, are you in there?"

"Mike just read the instructions. I'm in there, and there is a bunch of brown stuff oozing out; believe me you don't want to see it…but I bet you can smell it."

"Oh, man, this is too much. I'm *this close* to losing it. The brown stuff is what you have emptied, and it's what is causing old Max to drag his butt around. The smell is suffocating me—I need air. Wipe it up with paper towels—I'll get them—*anything* to get out of this stink box."

When Mike returned with the towels, he directed me, "Okay Ethan, wipe it all up and then shampoo the heck out of that butt."

"See what you're missing, Mike? Isn't this a 'walk in the park?' Seriously, the smell was a little daunting, and the thought of initially going in there was a bit disgusting, but I didn't really mind doing it…. Maybe I'm destined to be a vet!"

"Yeah, well, Ethan, I really have to get home now. It's unfortunate, but I think I'm going to be busy a lot over the next few weeks after school. Maybe we can hook up on the weekends, okay bud?"

"Yeah, Mikey, that's cool. Thanks for helping me with Max, but wait till my blog hears about what a wimp you are over a little anal gland clean up!" I taunted him.

"Oh, that's just great, Ethan, I'm so glad I'm such a good friend and came to help you out—*NOT!*"

"Go home, Mike, before I have to clean up vomit besides anal puss." Mike knew I was just "ragging" on him and he shut down his laptop and headed out the door, as fast as he could.

When Mr. Grant arrived, Max was thrilled to see him, and he got a satisfactory inspection.

"Ethan, I have to be honest, I was skeptical that someone your age would know how to express the anal glands of my dog. You have exceeded my expectations, and I hope this tip of fifteen dollars shows my gratitude. I may actually have a little marital bliss tonight when Mrs. Grant sees that Maxie is no longer dragging his butt all over our living room carpet. Thanks, Ethan."

"My pleasure, Mr. Grant. Your Max is a real sweetheart of a dog." As I shut the door, I wondered what incident I would make up to account for my mom's rubber gloves going missing...hmmm...

Blog of Day 9

Okay, my dedicated readers, I admit it, I am feeling somewhat smug tonight. Why you ask, would an amateur dog groomer be feeling this way? Well, I have to tell you that I performed a successful anal gland clean today on a Pug. As my trusty (and somewhat "grossed out") assistant referred to as emptying out or "expressing" the anal glands. That's correct my friends, this thirteen-year-old groomer performed a procedure during the bathing process that some people pay vets to do for them. Okay, so I feel successful tonight, so what? I'm sure my next humbling experience is just around the corner. As far as my best friend, I hope he has recovered from the "gross" ordeal that he witnessed, while reading the instructions to me from his laptop—you're the *man,* Mikey! Well, all my fellow French Bulldog lovers,

I am turning in early to gloat over my successful dog grooming venture of the day.

French Bulldog Fund: Day One $35.00

Day Two $35.00

Day Three $35.00

Day Four $40.00

TOTAL: $145.00

Determined and Entrepreneurial,
Frenchie's Best Friend

13

Thursday's Appointment

My mom *never ever* stays home from work, no matter how ill she may be. She believes it is her professional duty to be in front of her class each and every school day, and she has the same expectation of her family. Or at least that was true until I woke up on this particular morning. She came in and shook me awake. When I opened my eyes to groggily try to figure out what was happening, she pointed at her throat and made a slashing motion across it. Yep, she had laryngitis and absolutely couldn't squeak out a word. Now, normally, I would think this was kind of a relief, but not when she handed me a note.

Ethan, I have to stay home today and get my voice back. I feel really rotten, and there is no way I can manage twenty-eight students without a voice. You are going to have to call the Teacher-on-Call office for me. I'll dial and then you will have to read this to the prompts on the recording.

"This is Ethan Smith and I am calling for my mom, Clare Smith. She is ill today with laryngitis and she will need a TOC for the entire day. It is Oct. 6th and she has a Grade 4 class at Wascana School. She will email notes to the TOC to help her with the day plan."

As I made my way to the phone, I could feel my anxiety rise. What was I going to do now with Mom home and a Toy French Poodle coming in after school? My life just got super complicated in one fell swoop. I never expected my mom to get sick; that *NEVER EVER, EVER HAPPENS!* (Until today, that is!)

Of course, my conscientious mother, rather than going straight back to bed, was on the computer the entire time I was getting ready for school. She had to send detailed notes about each and every lesson and suggestions for working with some of her special students. This woman never lets up. She is truly the most Type A personality I know! Meanwhile, I was hyperventilating (inwardly, of course) knowing that I needed to get on the computer and try to reach the Poodle owner to postpone her appointment. But that wasn't going to happen, was it?

By the time I got to school, I thought I was going to throw up. Mike and the group saw me frantically approach and asked what had me going. When I explained my situation, they were empathetic of my predicament, but they all knew I couldn't chance checking my email account at school. We had all signed Internet usage agreements, and if I was caught breaking the agreement, my privileges would be revoked.

Jane was totally brilliant and came up with a plan instantly. She reminded me that the Strip Mall, a couple of blocks away from our Middle Years School, had an Internet café. It was agreed that I would head over there over the lunch break and send an email to the Poodle owner postponing the appointment. Of course, it still niggled at me, because there were no guarantees that the owner would check her emails before the afternoon appointment, but it was better than having no action plan at all.

At lunch, I tore over to the café, to find that every other person in the neighborhood had the same idea. At the last minute, before I had to run back to school, a computer freed up. When I checked my emails, my Friday appointment had cancelled and so I emailed the Poodle owner and suggested that she bring her dog tomorrow afternoon, rather than today. The minute I hit the Send button, I took off at top speed back to school, just as the last bell sounded. How I made it back in time is beyond me. To say I was "sweating bullets" would be an understatement. Our principal is super vigilant and if you are absent or late, your parents get a call immediately. How I would have explained this to my mother, I had no idea!

The rest of the school day was just a fog for me. I couldn't concentrate on anything, except what I was going to do if the client showed up after school and Mom found out about the grooming business. I didn't want to contemplate what would happen if that came to pass...my life wouldn't be worth living. If you haven't figured it out yet, my mom is somewhat of a formidable parent and *NO ONE* crosses her. My friends all recognized this about her and they could tell I was having a really bad day.

After the dismissal bell, I tore home to check my email. As I entered the house, guess who was sitting at the computer? Yep, you're right, there she was, totally immersed in curriculum planning in her pajamas. There was no way I was going to get a chance to check my emails!

"Hey, Mom, aren't you supposed to be in bed and getting better?" I asked.

"Ethan," she whispered, "I have been in bed all day. I can't just lie around anymore. Anyways, I think my voice is coming back, and I'll be back to work in the morning. So I'm getting my prep work done for tomorrow. Hey, I thought you'd be happy to see your old mom here when you got home today. It happens so rarely that I get to spend time with you right after you get home from school."

"I'm really glad that you're feeling better, Mom, but are you sure you should be working? Maybe you should just lie down, until I make us some dinner; soup might be the best bet, don't you think?"

"You are such a sweet boy, Ethan! (Boy she knows how to make me feel guilty!) I'm serious, I'm on the mend, so I'll just finish this off and then make *you* some dinner and give you a break from your duties. How does that sound?"

What could I say without raising her suspicions, so I said the only thing I could, "That would be great Mom, if you're absolutely sure that you should be doing all of that. While you finish your planning, I think I'll go over and give Cher a walk. Grandma really likes me to give her a little attention."

"Ethan, what a thoughtful guy you are. I'm so lucky to have such a wonderful son! You and Grandma seem pretty tight these days. If I didn't know better, I'd think you have a secret brewing between you," she remarked.

"Hey, Mom, you know Grandma Sis. She expects appropriate attention be paid to her on a regular basis. She's a character with her ways; that's for sure!" That's the best I could come up with. Mom has "acute antennae" and can pick up on things. I just wanted to have an excuse to get outside and wait there in case the Toy Poodle showed up. I had no other choice, as I certainly couldn't access my emails with my mom using the computer.

Of course my worst nightmare happened minutes later, as a cherry red Mercedes convertible pulled up and a fancy lady got out with her equally fancy Toy Poodle. I scurried over to the curb and explained my predicament.

"You must be Ms. Blanchard with your dog, Fou Fou. I'm Ethan, your dog's groomer. I'm so sorry to meet you out here, but we had a hot water tank leak earlier today and they're going to have to replace it. I tried to email you at lunch today to see if we could postpone Fou Fou's appointment until tomorrow, but I guess you didn't check your emails before coming over."

"*Mais non*, Ethan, I did not check my emails. *Mais oui*, we can wait until *demain* for Fou Fou's *bain*."

"I'm awfully sorry for the inconvenience this has caused you today, Ms. Blanchard, but I look forward to grooming Fou Fou tomorrow."

"*Bien*, Ethan. I am hopeful that you will be able to put the rouge streaks in Fou Fou's head puff and her pom pom tail. This is part of her grooming, *n'est-ce pas?*"

"*Ah, d'accord, Madame Blanchard. Au revoir et je vous vois demain!*" I couldn't believe that I, the Ethan that just barely passes French, had answered this customer *en français*. Let alone, what I had agreed to. I'm going to dye her Poodle's fur coat...how had this actually happened? Unbelievable! *Why don't these people read the flyers?!*

Of course, I tore over to Grandma Sis'. I can't say she looked overjoyed when she saw my face. She knew something was up, and it was going to have an impact on her. Unfortunately, she was in the middle of hosting a Tupperware party. I know what you're thinking, who does that in this day and age? Like I mentioned before, Grandma Sis is an entity all of her own!

"Ethan, you look flushed. Is there anything wrong?" she asked, as she noticed me come in.

"No, Grandma Sis, I'm sorry to interrupt your party. I just thought I would come over and take Cher for a walk, I know she could use some exercise."

"See what a darling boy Ethan is?" she commented to her friends. "Come on in the kitchen, Ethan, and I'll load you up on some squares to keep you going on your walk."

Grandma Sis is perceptive for an old woman. The minute we reached the kitchen, she whispered, "Okay, spill, what is really going on?"

I explained about Mom being sick and how I had to postpone the Poodle's appointment. Then I told her what Mme. Blanchard expected me to do. She could tell I was on the brink of hysteria.

"Okay, Ethan, settle down. This isn't the end of the world. I have red hair dye downstairs in my basement salon. I'm a hairdresser, after all. I will come over and help you tomorrow with the streaks. It shouldn't be a big deal. I must really love you, my boy, as it means I have to cancel my bridge party tomorrow and figure out an excuse to give Grandpa Bob for why I need to go and see you without raising suspicion. But you leave that to me. I'm a pro at this. (Don't I know it, if anyone can tell a "little white lie," it's Grandma Sis...) Tomorrow we'll make that little Foo Foo *très chaud*—that's French for *HOT,* Ethan!"

"*Je sais*, Grandma Sis; *je t'aime*. You've saved my life." (I couldn't help thinking how really cool my grandma is!)

"Don't be dramatic, Ethan; you just take Cher for that walk, *if* you can convince her to go anywhere near you..."

When I returned home, Mom already had dinner prepared before five-thirty (*totally* unheard of in our house). As I sat down to eat, she questioned me about the woman in the Mercedes that she noticed talking to me.

I took my "little white lie lessons" from Grandma Sis and answered, "Oh that. She was just someone who asked her way to the Strip Mall. She's new to the area and somehow took the wrong turn and then was completely lost. I was just giving her directions and having a look at her Toy Poodle."

I'm telling you, it had been a day; I was starting to feel like nothing that came out of my mouth was the truth anymore. I couldn't help but anticipate my mom's feelings when the truth finally came out and she knew the extent of my deception. *Would* she ever trust her son again? And *should* she ever trust him again?

Blog of Day 10

I am writing all of you tonight after an exhausting day of "dodging a bullet" and not having any additional income to record. That's right, you Frenchie lovers, it was a totally discombobulated day, right from the get-go. (I get my vocabulary skills from my mom, by the way. It's not that I am some super smart kid, but I do have vocab skills beyond expectations for my age.) My mom took an unprecedented sick day, I couldn't get hold of the client to postpone her dog's appointment, and then she lets me know that her Fou Fou (a very chic Miniature French Poodle) would require red streaks in her head poof and tail pom pom. I know what you're thinking: *Ethan, you know NOTHING whatsoever about hair/fur dyes. How are you going to fake your way through this one, right?* Oh, you are *so* right!! But I do have a grandma that still does her *little ladies'* hair in her basement. Thankfully, my grandmother is coming to the rescue, and we're going to apply red hair streaks to Fou Fou's white fur tomorrow after school. (It should have the same results on fur as it does on human hair, right?) Tomorrow is a new day; so glad my mom has her voice back and I can guarantee you she'll stay at work longer tomorrow after school because of losing a day; she is so predictable! Wish me luck with this high-end treatment. I figure I can charge an extra $35 for this (to make up for losing a client today). I better call my co-conspirator with a reminder of her commitment to join me for the dye job tomorrow—she sometimes forgets. Keep reading, my friends, it can only get more interesting…

French Bulldog Fund: **Day One** $35.00
                          Day Two $35.00
                          Day Three $35.00
                          Day Four $40.00
TOTAL: $145.00

Determined and Entrepreneurial,
Frenchie's Best Friend

Friday's Appointment

The day at school sped by like lightening. I think I was hoping school would never end, as I was feeling pretty apprehensive about working with dye on Mme. Blanchard's fancy French Poodle. I was smart enough to realize just how badly this could actually turn out.

When I arrived home, Grandma Sis surprised me by already being there to lend a hand. She had two different dyes with her—one a strawberry red and the other a burgundy red. Of course, I hadn't even considered that there would be a question of the color of red—DUH! She also had a plastic bonnet that had holes in it and a tool that looked like something from a fondue pot kit.

"Ethan, we have some prep work to do before your client gets here. You said that she wants streaks on her dog's tail pom pom? This cap won't work for that, so let's think about finding a small plastic bag that we can poke some holes in."

84

"Thanks, Grandma Sis, I know this isn't quite what you had in mind for your afternoon. You really are saving my life, here! What about a zip lock sandwich bag, would that work?" I asked.

"You know, I think it would be perfect as we could zip lock it or put an elastic around the tail pom pom. Go and get it, and I'll poke some holes in it with the bamboo stick I brought with me. Who says we aren't creative problem solvers?"

The doorbell rang at that very moment and, as I went to answer the door, Grandma slipped into the laundry room.

"*Bonjour Mme. Blanchard et Fou Fou.* Thanks for being so understanding yesterday about having to postpone your appointment," I apologized.

"*Mais oui,* Ethan. Fou Fou is ready for her beauty treatment. She wants to match my new Mercedes. *C'est possible, n'est-ce pas?*"

"*Mme. Blanchard,* I will do my best to get the color right. You want it just on her head puff and tail pom pom, right?"

"*Exactement,* Ethan! She has long toenails, but I think we will keep them this way for this treatment, as we *filles* love our nails. I will match some polish on them to complete her *très chic* look, *oui?*"

"Oh, *oui, oui, Mme. Blanchard.* I better get started, since you will be back to pick up Fou Fou by five-thirty, right?"

"Ethan, I thought I would just stay with my Fou Fou while you do her treatment. I love to see my Fou Fou getting fussed over."

"Oh *Mme. Blanchard,* it would be impossible for me to do this, as my shop is very cramped (All Grandma and I needed was someone watching us fumble our way through this one!). This would be a good opportunity for you to go out and try to find the nail polish that will match Fou Fou's new highlights."

"*Bien*, Ethan, *au revoir, ma belle Fou Fou.*" She slipped out the door, and I let out a huge sigh of relief.

Grandma Sis was poised beside the tub, getting ready to mix the chemicals for the streaks. "Okay Ethan, which one did she choose—the strawberry or the burgundy?" she inquired.

"Neither—she wants Fou Fou to match her new cherry red Mercedes—I'm not kidding!" I was exasperated. How were we going to deliver this one? I knew my Grandma Sis had some skills, but let's face it, there was a limit to what I assumed she was capable of delivering!

"Well, my boy, this complicates matters just a tad, doesn't it? Let's see, now, what will we do? I think the strawberry is closer to the cherry color, but it is lighter. I wonder if we mixed a small part of the burgundy paste in with it, whether it would deepen the color to a shade that would be close enough? Are you a risk-taker, Ethan? Let's give it a go."

"Grandma Sis, I'm leaving this up to you. You're the expert, here. I'm totally out of my depth on this one," I replied in frustration.

And so the mixing of chemicals began and the smell in the non-ventilated laundry room became nauseatingly overwhelming. Even poor Fou Fou started to gag.

"Ethan, you really have to toughen up. A little chemical won't kill you." (I wasn't so sure.) "Okay, let's fasten the cap on her head and tie it snugly. And then attach the zip lock bag to her tail. I brought an elastic, just in case the zip lock isn't tight enough."

I did as my grandma instructed. It was obvious that she was in charge, and I couldn't wait to get this ordeal over with.

"Okay, now, Ethan, you must use this hook and pull bits of fur through the holes. I'll hold Fou Fou, so she won't bite you while you torture her. That's right, she's going to hate this part more than the smell of the chemicals. Try to be gentle, but you have to get quite a few strands through for her to get the frosting color that your client wants," she instructed.

I picked up the hook and tried my first strand. Fou Fou snapped at me, and Grandma Sis just got her under control before she made contact with my wrist. Yikes, I had no idea this was going to be so painful for this little mutt. I felt like quitting, but of course I couldn't, so I tried the next one on the crown of her head. That strand came through a little easier. Let's just say, I could have NEVER done this on my own. Fou Fou would have attacked me and I would have lost my nerve. I kept going and, after what seemed forever, Grandma Sis told me I had enough done on her head and now to concentrate on her tail. This went a little faster, as it didn't seem to be such a sensitive area for poor Fou Fou, and she appeared less agitated and less ready to eat me!

"You know, Ethan, I don't think I could have done that better myself, maybe you have hairstyling genes from me. Now comes the fun part. I want you to paste the fur that you pulled out of the cap with this spatula. Put it on quite thickly and then we have to wait about ten minutes for it to set."

I followed Grandma's instructions under her watchful eye. She kept checking the solution on Fou Fou's head and then would make little "tsk, tsk" sounds. It was really getting on my nerves, but I dared not ask why she was doing it—I was too afraid of the answer. Finally, she announced it was time to take off the plastic caps and wash and condition Fou Fou's fur. I gently took the bags off—not as easy as it sounds, as the fur was matted on one side of the holes and had to go back through the holes to get them off. Fou Fou lost it at this point and started to growl and snarl, making me all the more jittery. Somehow, I got them off without Fou Fou attacking me and plopped her in the bath water. *Oh my gosh*, when I rinsed the soap out of Fou Fou's fur, I couldn't believe what I saw. Fou Fou had **PURPLE STREAKS**, she had **BRILLIANT DEEP PURPLE STREAKS**! Not exactly what I, let alone my client, had anticipated for her Poodle when she dropped Fou Fou off in my *NOT SO CAPABLE* hands!

"Grandma Sis, are those streaks the color I think they are?" I asked.

"Well, Ethan, I think it is fair to say that we have produced a unique shade of red; more exactly…purple, I'm not quite sure how I would describe it. I think you may have to sell the color to your client. Just finish up the blow dry and comb out, while I try to think just how we are going to spin this," she instructed.

I could tell that Grandma Sis was a little shaken; she was obviously as surprised by the color we had produced as I was. *IT WAS PURPLE!! Not* fire truck red, *not* apple red, and *definitely not Mercedes Convertible cherry red*—oh no—*IT WAS PURPLE*! We had single-handedly transformed the delicate French Poodle into a Goth dog!! Obviously, when Grandma mixed her concoction, she must have been a little heavy handed on the burgundy. I dreaded unveiling Fou Fou to Mme. Blanchard, I started to fret that she would sue me, and my mom would lose our house. Okay, I might have been overreacting, but you didn't see the color. Believe me, she wasn't going to have a matching nail polish for her fancy *chien* when she picked up her **PURPLE GOTH DOG**!

When I finished, there was about fifteen minutes left before Mme. Blanchard was expected. Grandma Sis snapped to attention. "Okay, my boy, your grandmother has the solution. You need to get on your bike and drive like "the speed of light" to the Dollar Store. Buy some of the red colored hair spray that they sell for Halloween, and such. We are going to give her a two-toned look. Now run, Ethan, the clock is ticking…"

You know how people say, "That person has horse shoes?" Well, that's the way I see what unfolded. There was an alignment of the stars. Somehow, I made it to the store, they had the cherry red colored hairspray in stock, and I returned exactly two minutes prior to the doorbell ringing. We had a minute to spray the ends of the purple streaks with the color that was more in keeping with Mme. Blanchard's dye request.

When I answered the door, I asked Grandma Sis to keep Fou Fou in the laundry room until I could prepare Mme. Blanchard for what I wanted to pass off as artistic autonomy and haute couture. I took a deep breath and plastered a confident smile on my face, as I opened the door.

"Ethan, am I too early? *Mais, où est ma chienne?* Look at the beautiful match I have for Fou Fou's nails—She will be *si belle*!

I confidently greeted her with, "*Mme. Blanchard*, I am very excited to present Fou Fou to you! I feel that I poured my creative juices into her coloring and came up with something so unique and *extraordinaire* that no other dog will come close to sporting a "doo" like Fou Fou's. Before I present her to you, I want to explain the creative license I took with her new look. She has steaks in her head poof and her tail pom pom, as you requested. These steaks are a unique deep purple, almost indescribable; much flashier than a mere cherry red. I have offset these trendy colored streaks with a simple colored hairspray, to be sprayed on every couple of days, to set off the tips with a red that is in complete agreement with your Mercedes red. The result is completely *magnifique* and such a fashion statement. I am sure you will agree!"

And with this, I opened the laundry room door with pomp and gusto as the very chic (or ruined, whichever way you spin it) Fou Fou pranced out with her head poof and tail pom pom proudly held high. Thank God that little mutt decided to cooperate. I watched Mme. Blanchard's facial expressions out of the corner of my eye. What I saw pass over her was sheer horror, replaced by bewilderment and, finally, a facial cover up that said she wasn't going to admit that this was a disaster and would accept and defend this as highly fashionable, no matter what.

"Oh, Ethan, my Fou Fou *est très, très unique!* She is *ma belle chienne.* You are a creative genius. Who would have thought of such a technique as two-toned streaks." she oozed.

I was on a roll and sensed I was out of danger, so I figured I better strike while I had the opportunity. "Well, Mme. Blanchard, I could tell you were a customer with discriminating taste and you had high expectations for Fou Fou's color treatment. I put a lot of effort to deliver something special for her. Of course, you do understand that for such a treatment, I will have to charge you fifty dollars on top of the twenty-five dollars for the bath." (Boy was I pushing my luck, but I had a feeling she was going to save face on this, no matter what!)

"Ethan, you have gone far and beyond my expectations. I have a hundred dollar bill *pour toi. Merci, mon chèr. Viens, ma belle chienne* Fou Fou."

The minute they were out the door, Grandma Sis bolted out of the laundry room and collapsed on the sofa in hysterics with me in her arms. We were overcome with disbelief that anyone could be so stupid as to tip me on such a debauchery. We couldn't help ourselves from imitating the poor woman. She obviously knew, in her heart of hearts, I had messed with her and her dog. When we finally came to our senses, I realized I had to get moving in order to be cleaned up before Mom came home and smelled the stench of those chemicals. But I was terribly curious and just had to ask Grandma Sis what she had told Grandpa Bob she was doing over here today.

She got a sly look on her face and said, "Well, Ethan I told him that you were thinking of getting a tattoo of your favorite breed of dog. So I said I was going to discourage you from mutilating your body with ink, by encouraging you to let me put a few streaks in your hair. You know Grandpa Bob. He thought that was a first-rate plan and was relieved that you would probably reconsider the tattoo. He still feels badly that your dad isn't able to be more involved in your day-to-day life and choices."

"You know, Grandma Sis, you are one creative woman—I can't believe the way you can come up with all of these stories!" I complimented her.

"Well, Ethan, watching Dr. Phil gives me all kinds of fodder for private conversations with my grandson, and a talk about "ink" seemed to be believable!"

Like I said, Grandma Sis likes to think she's on the cutting edge of coolness. She figures if she brings up any kind of current trends or topics (especially if they happen to be sex-related…), it reflects on her being "with it," as she puts it. One never knows what she might come out with next! At least this story was fairly tame, in the scheme of things.

Blog of Day 11

So, remember me saying that I was so glad to have many of the traits that Grandma Sis possesses? Well, I definitely had a firsthand experience today with her that makes me proud to be related to the woman. She really did manage to save the day and for that I am grateful. I can't help but laugh every time I visualize Fou Fou (the very chic French Poodle) prancing out of the laundry room with purple GOTH streaks on her head poof and tail pom pom. We used cherry red hairspray on the tips and sold it to the client as a very "in" look for dogs. Not only did the owner accept our nonsense, she gave me a hundred dollars for my creative genius! Okay, I admit it, I was really lucky to get away with it. Fou Fou looked ridiculous, and I truly thought the owner might resort to suing me. Am I going to ever dabble in fur dying again? Not on your life! (Grandma Sis reassures me that the streaks will eventually grow out and I'm sure Mme. Blanchard will *never* book another appointment with me!) However, the hundred dollars sure does put me ahead in my fund. I only wish I had had time to take a picture of Fou Fou to post on the web—you had to be there to appreciate the extent of the

ruse my Grandma and I pulled off today.
There is no question—the woman loves
scamming people! (How weird is that
for a grandma?)

I can't stop thinking about what
it will be like to have my very own
Frenchie. I think the business world
is taking a bit of a toll on my friend-
ships and definitely on my extra-cur-
ricular activities, but it is all going
to be worth it in the end—I'll have my
dog!

French Bulldog	Day One	$ 35.00
Fund:	Day Two	$ 35.00
	Day Three	$ 35.00
	Day Four	$ 40.00
	Day Five	$100.00
TOTAL:		$245.00

Determined and Entrepreneurial,
Frenchie's Best Friend

15

The Appointment from Hell

It's hard to believe that I've been managing this business through twenty appointments! Each and every customer has put me into a new learning experience. I finally became smarter and, after the first couple of weeks, I started to revise my bookings. They had to tell me the breed of their dog and *exactly* what they thought a wash entailed. You can appreciate why I had to adjust this, after some of the situations I had gotten myself into initially…You just have to remember Tiny…

And there have been so many close calls, where Mom almost figured out what was going on, but I think she's just so focused on her demanding class of twenty-eight kids that she actually doesn't want to face the reality that her son is doing something that she doesn't have complete control over. It's easier for her to "bury her head in the sand," than to search out what is happening right under her own nose. I'm not complaining. I think I'm lucky that my mom has a life and actually isn't micro-managing me the way some of my friends' parents do because they don't work and their kids are all they have to focus on. Just think, if Mom wasn't so preoccupied, I would never have had this opportunity to start my own business and save up for my Frenchie.

As I said, there've been several close calls, like the day she ran into Mike's mom at Safeway and they had a little chat. Mrs. Flannigan mentioned that Mike was a little disappointed that I didn't join the basketball team because I had so many extra responsibilities at home these days. My mom was speechless, and the minute she got in the door, she confronted me.

She demanded to know what Mike's mother meant. "Ethan, what in the world is Mrs. Flannigan talking about when she says that you couldn't play basketball this year because of all the extra responsibilities you were managing at home?"

I didn't see this coming, and I had to think really fast, "Oh that...yeah, well, Mike was driving me crazy about joining the team. You know how I like to play basketball for fun, but the new coach they hired this year is all about competition and winning. I figured I didn't really have a hope that he was going to give me a spot on the team, so I made up an excuse for not trying out. If I told Mike the real reason, he wouldn't let it go, and I would have had to go through the whole embarrassing ordeal of try-outs and being eliminated. It's okay for Mike; he's tall, and everyone wants the six-foot guys on the team, but for a height-challenged kid like me, it's a hopeless cause. So I made up a white lie and just said you were trying to develop my sense of responsibility and giving me more chores to do after school, because you were super busy with your class and taking your Master's night course."

She bought it and replied, "You know how I feel about white lies, Ethan. We have enough issues with that in our family without my son starting to take this up. I don't condone lying, no matter how innocent you think it is. I felt totally flabbergasted when she implied that I had kept you from joining the team and being with your friends."

"Mom, you know that isn't true. I like spending time with my friends on the weekend and you always let me do this. I was thinking about joining the Rec Centre basketball group, just for fun. I'd enjoy that a lot more, as it's just a 'fun league,' and I don't have to worry about letting my team members down. I'm really sorry I made you feel awkward with Mrs. Flannigan. I'll let Mike know the truth, so he can clear it up with her."

This was just one of the scenarios I had to deal with, and they always came out of left field. My mom is super busy and conscientious, but she prides herself on being a good mother who is on top of everything happening in her son's life. I totally fretted about the day when all of my deception would be uncovered, and I was going to have to deal with her reaction. I had a foreboding feeling it might not be pretty.

Besides all of the subterfuge issues with my mom, It amazed me how many people were reading my blog and trying to help me attain my goal with good advice and knowledge. I was so excited when I opened our mailbox after school yesterday and one of my readers had sent me a set of the plier-type nail clippers. I think he may have done this because of my Day 20 Blog, where I was expected to trim the nails of a cute little Shih-Tzu. He was most concerned about the damage I had the potential of doing and, like me, he didn't want to see *any* dog get hurt in my care. Of course, if my mom had any inkling that I had given out our address on my blog, I'd never be allowed on the computer again, unsupervised, for the rest of my life! It was a big risk, and I probably shouldn't have done it, in retrospect, but I could tell this was just someone who wanted me to do the right thing for the dogs and couldn't bear the thought that I might actually harm any of them. Although it was great to receive the package, I won't ever give that kind of info out on the web again. I actually know better. I'm just lucky it wasn't some pervert trying to get to know me personally; I really acted naively and, to be honest, I regret doing it; it just wasn't worth the worry.

Appointment 20

Yes, the Day 20 appointment was truly a memorable one. I was looking forward to working with the cute little Shih-Tzu after school and figured it was pretty much a regular wash, conditioner, and blow dry; quite within my comfort level. Of course, one should *NEVER* become complacent, because no appointment is just a regular; there is always something unique to the expectations of one's customers.

The day I opened the door to Brandy and her neurotic owner, I knew I was doomed. The dog itself was a nervous wreck, mostly because her owner was hyper-ventilating about every little detail.

"Please come in, Miss Connely. This must be Brandy." I welcomed them into the foyer. Brandy no sooner got into the vestibule, that she cowered and peed. *That's just great*, I thought, *now my mom would be smelling dog pee in the house all night!*

"Oh, excuse my little Brandy; she just gets so panicky coming to a new groomer. Of course with her beautiful show coat, I have to take her for trims constantly, so having a budget place for her bath and comb out in between made a lot of sense to me. It's so expensive these days keeping my Brandy looking so gorgeous," Miss Connely explained.

By now Brandy was whining and jumping on her owner's pant leg. "Don't give it another thought, Miss Connely," I responded. "You're right, I don't do dog trims, but she will have a great bath and blow dry."

At this point, Miss Connely had scooped up her Shih Tzu and was cradling her in her bare arms. She suddenly let out a yelp and dashed the dog to the floor as she brandished her damaged arm under my nose.

"Oh my little Brandy, her toenails grow so quickly, and they are incredibly sharp, just look at the damage she has done to my arm now! You do trim nails, right, Ethan? That's just a standard procedure with your bath service, right?"

I gulped thinking, *Here we go again! And I promised her that Brandy's nails would be trimmed. How I can come across so reassuring with clients when I'm feeling totally incompetent, I'll never understand.* Anyways, I showed her to the door, and then I sprang into action. First things first, this crazy little dog had to be isolated from the puddle she had created, before she stepped in it and tracked it all over Mom's carpets.

I picked up the whining Brandy and deposited her into the laundry room while I grabbed some paper towels and disinfectant to clean up her pee. I don't think I'll mind doing this for my Frenchie if he has the occasional accident, but I have to say, it makes my stomach heave to clean up after other people's dogs.

Anyways, the next order of business was to get back to the laundry room as soon as possible, because I could hear the neurotic Brandy starting to bark and scratch at the door.

I tore into my mom's bathroom and gathered her Pedi-Egg, emery board and nail scissors from her manicure set. What else could I do? I didn't have the proper dog clippers, and I wasn't going to be able to get out of this one.

I really did have Brandy sized up correctly. When I returned to the laundry room, she had already shredded one of my mom's dishcloths that had been hanging on the side of a pail under the sink. If I had left her for one more minute, who knew what damage she would have done?

Before she could demolish the laundry room, I scooped her up and set her into the bath. This dog really did have serious issues. As I started to rub in the shampoo, she began to quiver and tremble uncontrollably. I turned around to make sure I had the towels laid out, and when I turned back, I saw something foreign floating in the water... You know what it was, don't you? That little innocent princess, had *"laid a log"* right in the bath water. I could feel my sensitive stomach start to react. I couldn't believe it. I was going to have to pick it up and dispose of it. I grabbed the role of paper towels and held my nose with one hand while I picked up her poop. Of course, by being in the bath water, it was starting to get mushy and break apart. I finally got it contained in the towel and ran to the toilet to flush it down. Without even thinking, I flushed the wad of paper towels down with it. I couldn't give it another thought, as I had to get back to Brandy before she did anything else to ruin my day.

When I approached the bath, the cheeky little princess had the nerve to wag her prissy little tail at me.... "Are you kidding me, Brandy?" I yelled. Of course, this caused her to cower once again, and as I pulled the plug on the water, I wondered what else might be going down the drain.

Well, if I thought she was shivering before, she was totally freaked by having to stand in the tub while I refilled it. She was clawing at the sides, scrambling to get out and splashing water all over me and the surrounding floor and walls. All I could think about was how in the world I was going to keep her still, while I trimmed her nails. Of course, I had no experience or doggie tools to be doing this.

Somehow, I got her out of the rinse water and dried her coat with Mom's trusty blow dryer. She must have been accustomed to this, as she stood quite still during the process, once she had let loose of all the extra moisture by giving herself a shake in my face before I had a chance to unfold the towel. But what the heck, I was already totally soaked, what did it matter if I had yet another shower?

The whole time I was blow-drying the little princess, I was talking myself through how I thought I was going to trim her nails. I had watched my mom on countless Sunday nights give herself a pedicure in front of the TV after her bath (she rarely spent the money on a professional one). I figured I was going to have to do it the way we do human toenails and just be extra careful not to cut too much off. I knew about the issues around cutting the quick, which is the dog's nerve and blood vessels. My stomach couldn't take the sight of blood, that's for sure; the poop had already done me in! At least I was lucky to have a dog that had white nails as opposed to black ones, which would have been extra tricky to do.

I just kept telling myself that, like all other situations, I could do this. After all, I had cleaned the pug's anal glands, hadn't I? So, my big issue was going to be how to restrain Brandy from squirming while I managed the trimming. I figured a dog like her would probably respond well to positive reinforcement, so I opened the tin of doggie treats I had on hand. (Yes, I had given up on the Goldfish crackers and chocolate chips.)

As I flattened her tiny paw on the table and put the nail scissors in my hand, I was sweating buckets. My hand had a tremor like the alcoholics you see in movies who need a drink to calm their nerves. I had to speak severely to myself, "Get a grip, Ethan. You're going to go nice and easy and you will *not* hurt this little dog."

And that is exactly what I did. I took one nail at a time, and I cut just the curled over part of the nail with the scissors. Brandy was definitely a squirmer, and she didn't trust me (not that I could blame her), but I praised her profusely each time she let me take a trim off each nail and gave her a treat. I had read her well; she just basked in the attention and we got through the trimming without any major issues. Next, I took Mom's emery board and I filed away at the sharp edges. The nails were super hard, even though she had soaked them in the bath and this was more difficult. But…I did it and there wasn't any sign of blood or distress. I felt so thrilled with my work that I decided to treat her to some of Mom's new black nail lacquer. I was sure that Miss Connely would love it.

Now, this is where the horror show started. First of all, it's impossible to keep a dog calm enough to paint their nails. Secondly, black nail polish should never tip over. I'll leave you to your own imagination of the mess I created with that simple idea. Let's just say, I found out how to use nail polish remover real fast and Brandy had to go "au natural" after all.

By the time Miss Connely picked Brandy up, she was a nervous wreck wondering if she'd done the right thing leaving her precious princess with such a novice groomer. Thankfully, she didn't find out how I had trimmed Brandy's nails and there wasn't any evidence left on Brandy to indicate the aborted nail polishing faux pas.

As I closed the door on the little princess and her owner with my twenty-five dollars tightly clutched in my fist, I couldn't help think, *I am so done! I've got to get my own dog soon!*

Just before Mom arrived home from her class, I used the washroom that I had flushed the wad of extra strength paper towels down. *BIG BIG MISTAKE!* I had an overflowing toilet bowl with my mom about to appear at any minute.

Thankfully, I had Grandma Sis to count on. She's never flustered and told me all about the plunger that every household has. Sure enough, there was one in the laundry room closet and it worked. The wad of paper towels surfaced and I retrieved them for the garbage can. My poor delicate stomach really took a beating; a plumber I could never be!

How I got everything cleaned before my mom walked in that night, I'll never know. Between the black nail polish and the plugged toilet, I was completely done in!

Blog of Day 20

I'm so finished tonight, I can hardly send out this blog. I am seriously learning so much about people and their dogs, these days—maybe too much! Today's customer was a neurotic woman with an equally bizarre Shih-Tzu. What I thought was going to be a regular bath and comb out, turned into a frenzy of craziness. The dog couldn't be left a second unsupervised without destroying property by peeing, pooping, and tearing things apart. I know you probably think this is funny…NOT! I had to take dog poo out of her bath water and then I plugged the toilet because I flushed down a wad of paper towels…the madness just went on and on. Anyways, the biggest trial was that this woman wanted me to trim her dog's nails. Now you and I both know that I haven't got a hot clue how to go about this. Once again, I had to improvise, but I was so scared I was going to make the poor wreck of a dog bleed that I had the shakes just trying to do the procedure with my mom's nail scissors and emery board. Sometimes, I think I am just too much. I got through the trimming without a fatality, but then, I had this stupid idea that I should put my mom's new black polish on her nails. Let's just say that was the "icing on the cake"—what a mess I had to clean up. I'm sure by now you have gotten the gist of the appointment from HELL! And to top it off, she didn't even tip me, can you believe it?! I just have to go to bed and forget this day ever happened!

French Bulldog Fund:		
	Day One	$ 35.00
	Day Two	$ 35.00
	Day Three	$ 35.00
	Day Four	$ 40.00
	Day Five	$100.00
	Day Six	$ 35.00
	Day Seven	$ 35.00
	Day Eight	$ 25.00
	Day Nine	$ 35.00
	Day Ten	$ 35.00

Day Eleven	$ 40.00
Day Twelve	$ 30.00
Day Thirteen	$ 35.00
Day Fourteen	$ 35.00
Day Fifteen	$ 40.00
Day Sixteen	$ 25.00
Day Seventeen	$ 25.00
Day Eighteen	$ 30.00
Day Nineteen	$ 35.00
Day Twenty	$ 25.00

TOTAL: $730.

(Looking at this makes me feel better!)

Determined and Entrepreneurial,
Frenchie's Best Friend

16

Frenchie Lovers Unite Through Social Networking

Christmas was fast approaching, and I was getting really desperate to own my Frenchie. I had been scouring the Internet sites chatting with breeders to see what puppies were available and the costs to be incurred. Every time I would find one I would tear over to Grandma Sis' and we'd work it through. I have to admit, that for all of our bravado when we decided to get our plan underway, we were both feeling nervous about the "day of reckoning" when Mom would be faced with a puppy in her house and we'd have to explain how it got there. As Grandma Sis put it, "I'm in a bit of a tight spot, Ethan. She is your mom, so she'll forgive you because of a mother's unconditional love, no matter what craziness you get yourself into. I, on the other hand, am your father's mother, and she is much more inclined to take my involvement as interference. She may even decide to disown me!"

As the holidays approached, my appointments had really dropped off. Most people are super busy prior to the holiday season and they were probably making appointments for their dogs at the more professional doggie spas. I had already informed my clients that I would not be taking any bookings over the holidays. Of course, they wouldn't know this was because my mom would be around. To be honest, I was looking forward to a little free time. My life had been pretty intense since I went into business for myself. I had a total of $1260, which made me feel quite rich, but realistically in pure-bred dog terms, this was just a "drop in the bucket." It was definitely going to take me longer than I ever thought to make the kind of cash I needed to own my own Frenchie.

My readers were still involved in my blog and continued to support my efforts, but out of nowhere came a "gift" I had not anticipated. I couldn't believe my eyes when I read what was posted on my blog!

Hi Determined and Entrepreneurial,

I'm a French Bulldog breeder and have enjoyed following your journey over the last three months. It has not only been amusing, but it has told me a lot about you as a person and a potential owner of my favored breed. I'm a reputable breeder, impressed by your perseverance to earn your dog, taking into consideration that there will be expenses and responsibili-

ties through becoming a French Bulldog owner.

It is obvious to me that you have a lot of love to give your dog and that you are determined to have the best breed of dog in the world—the funny and loving French Bulldog!

I have a new litter of five puppies. There is one darling little female that is the runt of the litter. This means that she won't be a dog that people will purchase for show or breeding, even though she comes from a pedigree of winners. She is small, but probably the most personable puppy I have ever had. She is five weeks old and I will be willing to let her go to a great home by Christmas Eve, with her shots completed and a clean bill of health from our vet. She will have cost me approximately seven hundred dollars, and I would have to ship her out to you by air for about $250.

What I am trying to say is that I am offering you this adorable female puppy for the cost of my expenses. Now, I know she may not be exactly what you were considering, but I think you would give her a wonderful home and hope you will consider this little cream cutie. From reading your blog, I'd say the two of you were made for each other! Take a look at her picture that I have sent along with this and tell me you could say no my generous offer!

Jean Austin
Magnifique French Bulldog Kennels

Unbelievable, it was like love at first sight. How could any puppy be that adorable?! All of my fantasies of having this macho, cocky, black, male Frenchie went completely out the window as I took in the picture of this incredible cutie.

I quickly printed off the picture and the breeder's letter. I had to get this over to Grandma Sis' to see what she thought. I was already thinking about her arrival on Christmas Eve and what it would be like to have her arrive as my Christmas present. That was it. I knew how I was going to get around my mom. If this puppy was presented as a Christmas gift, how could she possibly refuse to let me keep it? I had to get over to Grandma's—this was meant to be.

Come to Ethan

Blog of Day 32

Well everyone, by now you know that my goal to own a French Bulldog has come to fruition. Thanks to the generous offer of Magifique French Bulldog Breeders, my little cream beauty is arriving on the Westjet Flight from Kamloops at two-thirty on Christmas Eve. Grandma Sis is still a little apprehensive about Mom's reaction, but she loves a deal and the fact that we only had to pay for expenses really appealed to her. I'm being harsh; of course, Grandma Sis has a soft heart and she couldn't refuse that darling little face any more than I could. It's funny, my little "Sissy" isn't at all the macho Frenchie I had in mind. First of all, she's female, cream—not black, and she's tiny, not a heavy, hulking mass of bulk. But it is love, that's all I can say. As soon as I saw that cute little face, I knew she had to be mine. There are three more days before she's shipped out here and Grandma Sis and I are trying to figure out the logistics of telling my mom. This is no simple matter and we are both cowards!

Since my dad moved on and made his home in Victoria, my mom and I spend Christmas Eve with Grandma Sis and Grandpa Bob, after Mom entertains some of her friends with an open house in the afternoon. Then the next morning, I head out with Grandma and Grandpa to Victoria for Christmas dinner with my dad, and Mom gets together with her sister's family in White Rock. So, this is how we anticipate it's all going to unfold. While Mom is entertaining her friends, I'm going to sneak out to go to the airport with Grandma Sis and we'll pick up "Sissy" (yes, named after my partner in crime—Grandma Sis and also because she is the opposite of my macho vision of a dog). Sissy will stay hidden in Grandma Sis' basement (we have her little bed all fixed up) until we exchange our gifts. That's when Sissy is going to make her appearance. Grandpa Bob has been brought up to speed, so he can help with the logistics. Hopefully, he won't spill the beans. He and Grandma really have a problem with keeping secrets; it drives me nuts!

We think the holiday season and good cheer will work to our advantage. Once Mom knows everything, surely she will be okay with it. After all, she isn't going to want to look like *the Grinch* on Christmas Eve! Grandma Sis says if the worst comes to pass, she and Grandpa Bob will keep Sissy with Cher. (I think my grandma is just a little smitten already by her namesake!) Of course, I can't bear to think that my mom could actually not let this little cutie melt her heart and welcome her to the family. Wish me luck, dear readers. I have to admit, I'm getting beyond excited. If Mom can't tell something is brewing, she must really be on overload from report cards, Christmas concerts, and her major paper for her Master's class. We hardly even encounter one another these days; she has been so busy. Maybe that's working in my favor for a change. All I can say is "keep the faith" my Frenchie lovers!

Determined and Entrepreneurial,
Frenchie's Best Friend

Blog of Day 33

Well, my friends, we are exactly three hours away from my final blog and the finale of my entire adventure to become a French Bulldog owner. Sissy will be boarding the plane in about an hour, and Grandma Sis and I have everything ready for her—of course it's all over at Grandma's place. Mom is in a great mood today. She's been humming Christmas carols, as she prepares for her afternoon party. I know she loves Christmas, and she mostly loves the present exchange when she thinks she has really surprised me with something special. I think the surprise is going to be on her this year!

My final blog will be posted later tonight, with my little Sissy curled up in my lap—I hope! Keep the faith Brothers and Sisters, and Merry Christmas to all of you believers.

Determined and Entrepreneurial,
Frenchie's Best Friend

18

The Plan Comes Full Circle–Or Almost

Final Blog of Day 33

Well everyone, I know you have waited all night to hear the outcome of the unveiling of my beautiful little Sissy. Let's just say it didn't exactly go according to *"the plan."* This shouldn't surprise any of us, as not much from the get-go of this adventure has gone the way I anticipated. I'm not complaining, believe me, but I do have a tale to tell.

As previously mentioned, Grandma Sis was going to take me to the airport, just as soon as I could disappear from Mom's Open House without being noticed. That proved a little unnerving, as Mom kept asking me to be the official server. However, once everyone was well into the party mode, I quietly extricated myself out the garage door and literally flew over to Grandma Sis' house.

She had the car backed out of the garage and we drove straight to the airport. Because it had taken me a bit longer to get out of my house undetected, we were a few minutes late. When we arrived at the baggage area, there was a crowd "oohing and ahhing" in front of an animal crate. You guessed it, everyone was totally infatuated with the darling little Frenchie who was trying to reach her fans with her over-active tongue. My first reaction was that she was more adorable than I had ever imagined. She took to Grandma Sis and me right from the minute we laid eyes on her.

We got her home to Grandma Sis' safe and sound and, can you believe it, she even took a little squat and peed outside before going into the house? That really impressed my Grandma Sis, I can tell you. Of course, I was struggling with tearing myself away from my Frenchie that I had waited so long to realize. However, Grandma Sis knew I had no choice, so she practically had to steer me to the door so that I could sneak back home without my mom being any the wiser. It was so hard to leave Sissy behind!

Anyways, I did return home, made it in without raising anyone's curiosity about where I had disappeared. Everyone expects teenagers to leave their parents' social gatherings to mope in their bedrooms on the Internet, right?

Finally, Mom's friends left, and we quickly tidied up and got ready to go to Grandma and Grandpa's with our gifts. Unbeknownst to Mom, I had called Grandma Sis at least six times in the last hour for an update on my puppy. I just couldn't get over there soon enough.

We always have a special Christmas Eve dinner with turkey and tourtières. The meal seemed to be excruciatingly long and, every once in awhile, I would excuse myself to get more gravy or visit the washroom. Of course, I was actually just checking up on Sissy.

She would attack me with kisses every time I reached in to pick her up.

At one point, there was puppy crying coming from the basement and my mom stopped mid-sentence and asked, "What is going on with Cher—I've never heard her make that kind of sound before!"

Grandma Sis just sloughed it off with another white lie. "That little Cher is being very spoiled today. She got into the stuffing that I had set out on the deck to cool off and so she got a little smack. Now she's carrying on like a baby—she'll get over it if we just ignore her." That's my Grandma Sis. She can truly think on her feet and the little white lies just flow off her tongue.

Finally, dessert was served and then the table was cleared. This set the scene for Sissy's big entrance, but before Grandpa Bob could make it happen...Mom realized she had left an important present at home by mistake and insisted she had to go home and get it. The clock was ticking so slowly we didn't think she was ever going to return...

When we finally heard the door open, instead of Mom walking through the door, a heavyset, spirited, and the most macho "little man" strode into the living room and lifted his leg on Grandma Sis' chair leg. We were aghast, where had this Frenchie of my dreams come from? We were all so mesmerized that the shock of his cocked leg threw us all into convulsions. My mom followed this brazen puppy in and announced, "MERRY CHRISTMAS ETHAN!" We were dumbfounded, and everyone went completely silent. This is the point when Sissy decided to step her whimpering up a notch, and Grandpa Bob sprang into action. Two seconds later, Sissy dashed in and jumped up on the foreign black Frenchie and gave him a few quick licks. I found my voice and announced, "MERRY CHRISTMAS, MOM!"

We both collapsed next to the puppies and gave each other the "how did this happen?" look. I let my mom explain first. (I still wasn't confident that she'd be happy with my story!)

As it turned out, she had been planning this surprise for quite awhile. Apparently one of the kids in her class adopted a dog through a rescue network. It had turned out really well for the family, so Mom did some research and found a French Bulldog Rescue Network, and when she found Pierre, she knew she had to make it happen. It was the precise dog that I had been describing as my "dream dog" *forever.* My mom's face just glowed, as she told her story and saw my surprise and happiness. But then the tables turned and she asked me to explain "Sissy."

Remember, how I said that one of my strengths is that I'm a fast thinker? Well, tonight was the ultimate. I explained that I had realized that my mom needed something to love, even if she wouldn't admit it. So I had made a great sacrifice and started a business to enable me to purchase the cutest little Frenchie girl I could find (I know, you're thinking that I'm getting too good at these little white lies…). Anyways, it was obvious that Mom couldn't take her eyes off Sissy and that she had already fallen for her. The rest of the story came out gradually in dribs and drabs and, by the time we left Grandma and Grandpa's with our two Frenchie babies, we were both euphoric about our expanded family.

Now, dear reader, you may be wondering where Sissy and Pierre are while I'm writing my final blog. They have both curled up in their special bed at my feet and are snoring in harmony—it is music to my ears.

Who says dreams can't come true? This has been the best Christmas ever, and I can hardly wait for my new adventure to unfold as Mom and I raise our two beautiful puppies together. Somehow, I have the distinct feeling that reality might set in rather quickly, hmmm…. Maybe there is yet another blog to be written….

Determined and Entrepreneurial,
Frenchie's Best Friend

8109194R0